THE SCARECROW WALKS AT MIDNIGHT

Look for more Goosebumps books by R.L. Stine:

Goosebumps

THE SCARECROW WALKS AT MIDNIGHT

R.L. STINE

AN
APPLE
PAPERBACK

SCHOLASTIC INC.
New York Toronto London Auckland Sydney

No part of this publication may be reproduced in whole or in part, or stored in a retrieval system, or transmitted in any form or by any means, electronic, mechanical, photocopying, recording, or otherwise, without written permission of the publisher. For information regarding permission, write to Scholastic Inc., 555 Broadway, New York, NY 10012.

ISBN 0-590-47742-0

12   5 6 7 8 9/9

Printed in the U.S.A.   40

First Scholastic printing, May 1994

1

"Hey, Jodie — wait up!"

I turned and squinted into the bright sunlight. My brother, Mark, was still on the concrete train platform. The train had clattered off. I could see it snaking its way through the low, green meadows in the distance.

I turned to Stanley. Stanley is the hired man on my grandparents' farm. He stood beside me, carrying both suitcases. "Look in the dictionary for the word 'slowpoke,' " I said, "and you'll see Mark's picture."

Stanley smiled at me. "I like the dictionary, Jodie," he said. "Sometimes I read it for hours."

"Hey, Mark — get a move on!" I cried. But he was taking his good time, walking slowly, in a daze as usual.

I tossed my blond hair behind my shoulders and turned back to Stanley. Mark and I hadn't visited the farm for a year. But Stanley still looked the same.

He's so skinny. "Like a noodle," my grandma always says. His denim overalls always look five sizes too big on him.

Stanley is about forty or forty-five, I think. He wears his dark hair in a crewcut, shaved close to his head. His ears are huge. They stick way out and are always bright red. And he has big, round, brown eyes that remind me of puppy eyes.

Stanley isn't very smart. Grandpa Kurt always says that Stanley isn't working with a full one hundred watts.

But Mark and I really like him. He has a quiet sense of humor. And he is kind and gentle and friendly, and always has lots of amazing things to show us whenever we visit the farm.

"You look nice, Jodie," Stanley said, his cheeks turning as red as his ears. "How old are you now?"

"Twelve," I told him. "And Mark is eleven."

He thought about it. "That makes twenty-three," he joked.

We both laughed. You never know *what* Stanley is going to say!

"I think I stepped in something gross," Mark complained, catching up to us.

I *always* know what Mark is going to say. My brother only knows three words — *cool, weird,* and *gross.* Really. That's his whole vocabulary.

As a joke, I gave him a dictionary for his last birthday. "You're *weird,*" Mark said when I handed it to him. "What a *gross* gift."

2

He scraped his white high-tops on the ground as we followed Stanley to the beat-up, red pickup truck. "Carry my backpack for me," Mark said, trying to shove the bulging backpack at me.

"No way," I told him. "Carry it yourself."

The backpack contained his Walkman, about thirty tapes, comic books, his Game Boy, and at least fifty game cartridges. I knew he planned to spend the whole month lying on the hammock on the screened-in back porch of the farmhouse, listening to music and playing video games.

Well . . . no way!

Mom and Dad said it was *my* job to make sure Mark got outside and enjoyed the farm. We were so cooped up in the city all year. That's why they sent us to visit Grandpa Kurt and Grandma Miriam for a month each summer — to enjoy the great outdoors.

We stopped beside the truck while Stanley searched his overall pockets for the key. "It's going to get pretty hot today," Stanley said, "unless it cools down."

A typical Stanley weather report.

I gazed out at the wide, grassy field beyond the small train station parking lot. Thousands of tiny white puffballs floated up against the clear blue sky.

It was so beautiful!

Naturally, I sneezed.

I love visiting my grandparents' farm. My only

problem is, I'm allergic to just about everything on it.

So Mom packs several bottles of my allergy medicine for me — and lots of tissues.

"*Gesundheit*," Stanley said. He tossed our two suitcases in the back of the pickup. Mark slid his backpack in, too. "Can I ride in back?" he asked.

He loves to lie flat in the back, staring up at the sky, and bumping up and down really hard.

Stanley is a terrible driver. He can't seem to concentrate on steering and driving at the right speed at the same time. So there are always lots of quick turns and heavy bumps.

Mark lifted himself into the back of the pickup and stretched out next to the suitcases. I climbed beside Stanley in the front.

A short while later, we were bouncing along the narrow, twisting road that led to the farm. I stared out the dusty window at the passing meadows and farmhouses. Everything looked so green and alive.

Stanley drove with both hands wrapped tightly around the top of the steering wheel. He sat forward stiffly, leaning over the wheel, staring straight ahead through the windshield without blinking.

"Mr. Mortimer doesn't farm his place anymore," he said, lifting one hand from the wheel to point to a big, white farmhouse on top of a sloping, green hill.

"Why not?" I asked.

"Because he died," Stanley replied solemnly.

See what I mean? You never know what Stanley is going to say.

We bounced over a deep rut in the road. I was sure Mark was having a great time in back.

The road leads through the small town, so small that it doesn't even have a name. The farmers have always called it Town.

It has a feed store, a combination gas station and grocery store, a white-steepled church, a hardware store, and a mailbox.

There were two trucks parked in front of the feed store. I didn't see anyone as we barreled past.

My grandparents' farm is about two miles from town. I recognized the cornfields as we approached.

"The corn is so high already!" I exclaimed, staring through the bouncing window. "Have you eaten any yet?"

"Just at dinner," Stanley replied.

Suddenly, he slowed the truck and turned his eyes to me. "The scarecrow walks at midnight," he uttered in a low voice.

"Huh?" I wasn't sure I'd heard correctly.

"The scarecrow walks at midnight," he repeated, training his big puppy eyes on me. "I read it in the book."

I didn't know what to say, so I laughed. I thought maybe he was making a joke.

Days later, I realized it was no joke.

2

Watching the farm spread out in front of us filled me with happiness. It's not a big farm or a fancy farm, but I like everything about it.

I like the barn with its sweet smells. I like the low mooing sounds of the cows way off in the far pasture. I like to watch the tall stalks of corn, all swaying together in the wind.

Corny, huh?

I also like the scary ghost stories Grandpa Kurt tells us at night in front of the fireplace.

And I have to include Grandma Miriam's chocolate chip pancakes. They're so good, I sometimes dream about them back home in the city.

I also like the happy expressions on my grandparents' faces when we come rushing up to greet them.

Of course I was the first one out of the truck. Mark was as slow as usual. I went running up to the screen porch in back of their big, old farmhouse. I couldn't *wait* to see my grandparents.

Grandma Miriam came waddling out, her arms outstretched. The screen door slammed behind her. But then I saw Grandpa Kurt push it open and he hurried out, too.

His limp was worse, I noticed right away. He leaned heavily on a white cane. He'd never needed one before.

I didn't have time to think about it as Mark and I were smothered in hugs. "So good to see you! It's been so long, so long!" Grandma Miriam cried happily.

There were the usual comments about how much taller we were and how grown up we looked.

"Jodie, where'd you get that blond hair? There aren't any blonds in *my* family," Grandpa Kurt would say, shaking his mane of white hair. "You must get that from your father's side.

"No, I know. I bet you got it from a store," he said, grinning. It was his little joke. He greeted me with it every summer. And his blue eyes would sparkle excitedly.

"You're right. It's a wig," I told him, laughing.

He gave my long blond hair a playful tug.

"Did you get cable yet?" Mark asked, dragging his backpack along the ground.

"Cable TV?" Grandpa Kurt stared hard at Mark. "Not yet. But we still get three channels. How many more do we need?"

Mark rolled his eyes. "No MTV," he groaned.

Stanley made his way past us, carrying our suitcases into the house.

"Let's go in. I'll bet you're starving," Grandma Miriam said. "I made soup and sandwiches. We'll have chicken and corn tonight. The corn is very sweet this year. I know how you two love it."

I watched my grandparents as they led the way to the house. They both looked older to me. They moved more slowly than I remembered. Grandpa Kurt's limp was definitely worse. They both seemed tired.

Grandma Miriam is short and chubby. She has a round face surrounded by curly red hair. Bright red. There's no way to describe the color. I don't know what she uses to dye it that color. I've never seen it on anyone else!

She wears square-shaped eyeglasses that give her a really old-fashioned look. She likes big, roomy housedresses. I don't think I've ever seen her in jeans or pants.

Grandpa Kurt is tall and broad-shouldered. Mom says he was really handsome when he was young. "Like a movie star," she always tells me.

Now he has wavy, white hair, still very thick, that he wets and slicks down flat on his head. He has sparkling blue eyes that always make me smile. And a white stubble over his slender face. Grandpa Kurt doesn't like to shave.

8

Today he was wearing a long-sleeved, red-and-green-plaid shirt, buttoned to the collar despite the hot day, and baggy jeans, stained at one knee, held up by white suspenders.

Lunch was fun. We sat around the long kitchen table. Sunlight poured in through the big window. I could see the barn in back and the cornfields stretching behind it.

Mark and I told all our news — about school, about my basketball team going to the championships, about our new car, about Dad growing a mustache.

For some reason, Stanley thought that was very funny. He was laughing so hard, he choked on his split-pea soup. And Grandpa Kurt had to reach over and slap him on the back.

It's hard to know what will crack Stanley up. As Mark would say, Stanley is definitely *weird*.

All through lunch, I kept staring at my grandparents. I couldn't get over how much they had changed in one year. They seemed so much quieter, so much slower.

That's what it means to get older, I told myself.

"Stanley will have to show you his scarecrows," Grandma Miriam said, passing the bowl of potato chips. "Won't you, Stanley?"

Grandpa Kurt cleared his throat loudly. I had the feeling he was telling Grandma Miriam to change the subject or something.

"I made them," Stanley said, grinning proudly. He turned his big eyes on me. "The book — it told me how."

"Are you still taking guitar lessons?" Grandpa Kurt asked Mark.

I could see that, for some reason, Grandpa Kurt didn't want to talk about Stanley's scarecrows.

"Yeah," Mark answered with a mouthful of potato chips. "But I sold my acoustic. I switched to electric."

"You mean you have to plug it in?" Stanley asked. He started to giggle, as if he had just cracked a funny joke.

"What a shame you didn't bring your guitar," Grandma Miriam said to Mark.

"No, it isn't," I teased. "The cows would start giving sour milk!"

"Shut up, Jodie!" Mark snapped. He has no sense of humor.

"They already *do* give sour milk," Grandpa Kurt muttered, lowering his eyes.

"Bad luck. When cows give sour milk, it means bad luck," Stanley declared, his eyes widening, his expression suddenly fearful.

"It's okay, Stanley," Grandma Miriam assured him quickly, placing a hand gently on his shoulder. "Grandpa Kurt was only teasing."

"If you kids are finished, why not go with Stanley," Grandpa Kurt said. "He'll give you a tour of the farm. You always enjoy that." He sighed. "I'd

10

go along, but my leg — it's been acting up again."

Grandma Miriam started to clear the dishes. Mark and I followed Stanley out the back door. The grass in the back yard had recently been mowed. The air was heavy with its sweet smell.

I saw a hummingbird fluttering over the flower garden beside the house. I pointed it out to Mark, but by the time he turned, it had hummed away.

At the back of the long, green yard stood the old barn. Its white walls were badly stained and peeling. It really needed a paint job. The doors were open, and I could see square bales of straw inside.

Far to the right of the barn, almost to the cornfields, stood the small guest house where Stanley lived with his teenage son, Sticks.

"Stanley — where's Sticks?" I asked. "Why wasn't he at lunch?"

"Went to town," Stanley answered quietly. "Went to town, riding on a pony."

Mark and I exchanged glances. We never can figure Stanley out.

Poking up from the cornfield stood several dark figures, the scarecrows Grandma Miriam had started to talk about. I stared out at them, shielding my eyes from the sun with one hand.

"So many scarecrows!" I exclaimed. "Stanley, last summer there was only one. Why are there so many now?"

He didn't reply. He didn't seem to hear me. He

had a black baseball cap pulled down low over his forehead. He was taking long strides, leaning forward with that storklike walk of his, his hands shoved into the pockets of his baggy denim overalls.

"We've seen the farm a hundred times," Mark complained, whispering to me. "Why do we have to take the grand tour again?"

"Mark — cool your jets," I told him. "We *always* take a tour of the farm. It's a tradition."

Mark grumbled to himself. He really is lazy. He never wants to do anything.

Stanley led the way past the barn into the cornfields. The stalks were way over my head. Their golden tassels gleamed in the bright sunlight.

Stanley reached up and pulled an ear off the stalk. "Let's see if it's ready," he said, grinning at Mark and me.

He held the ear in his left hand and started to shuck it with his right.

After a few seconds, he pulled the husk away, revealing the ear of corn inside.

I stared at it — and let out a horrified cry.

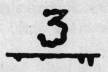

3

"Ohhhh — it's *disgusting*!" I shrieked.

"Gross!" I heard Mark groan.

The corn was a disgusting brown color. And it was *moving* on the cob. Wriggling. Squirming.

Stanley raised the corn to his face to examine it. And I realized it was covered with worms. Hundreds of wriggling, brown worms.

"No!" Stanley cried in horror. He let the ear of corn drop to the ground at his feet. "That's bad luck! The book says so. That's very bad luck!"

I stared down at the ear of corn. The worms were wriggling off the cob, onto the dirt.

"It's okay, Stanley," I told him. "I only screamed because I was surprised. This happens sometimes. Sometimes worms get into the corn. Grandpa told me."

"No. It's bad," Stanley insisted in a trembling voice. His red ears were aflame. His big eyes revealed his fear. "The book — it says so."

"What book?" Mark demanded. He kicked the

13

wormy ear of corn away with the toe of his high-top.

"My book," Stanley replied mysteriously. "My superstition book."

Uh-oh, I thought. Stanley shouldn't have a book about superstitions. He was already the most superstitious person in the world — even without a book!

"You've been reading a book about superstitions?" Mark asked him, watching the brown worms crawl over the soft dirt.

"Yes." Stanley nodded his head enthusiastically. "It's a good book. It tells me everything. And it's all true. All of it!"

He pulled off his cap and scratched his stubby hair. "I've got to check the book. I've got to see what to do about the corn. The bad corn."

He was getting pretty worked up. It was making me feel a little scared. I've known Stanley my whole life. I think he's worked for Grandpa Kurt for more than twenty years.

He's always been strange. But I've never seen him get so upset about something as unimportant as a bad ear of corn.

"Show us the scarecrows," I said, trying to get his mind off the corn.

"Yeah. Let's see them," Mark joined in.

"Okay. The scarecrows." Stanley nodded. Then he turned, still thinking hard, and began leading the way through the tall rows of cornstalks.

14

The stalks creaked and groaned as we passed by them. It was kind of an eerie sound.

Suddenly, a shadow fell over me. One of the dark scarecrows rose up in front of us. It wore a tattered black coat, stuffed with straw. Its arms stretched stiffly out at its sides.

The scarecrow was tall, towering over my head. Tall enough to stand over the high cornstalks.

Its head was a faded burlap bag, filled with straw. Evil black eyes and a menacing frown had been painted on thickly in black paint. A battered old-fashioned hat rested on its head.

"You made these?" I asked Stanley. I could see several other scarecrows poking up from the corn. They all stood in the same stiff position. They all had the same menacing frown.

He stared up the scarecrow's face. "I made them," he said in a low voice. "The book showed me how."

"They're pretty scary looking," Mark said, standing close beside me. He grabbed the scarecrow's straw hand and shook it. "What's up?" Mark asked it.

"The scarecrow walks at midnight," Stanley said, repeating the phrase he had used at the train station.

Mark was trying to slap the scarecrow a high-five.

"What does that *mean*?" I asked Stanley.

"The book told me how," Stanley replied, keeping his eyes on the dark-painted face on the burlap bag. "The book told me how to make them walk."

"Huh? You mean you make the scarecrows *walk?*" I asked, very confused.

Stanley's dark eyes locked on mine. Once again, he got that very solemn expression on his face. "I know how to do it. The book has all the words."

I stared back at him, totally confused. I didn't know what to say.

"I made them walk, Jodie," Stanley continued in a voice just above a whisper. "I made them walk last week. And now I'm the boss."

"Huh? The boss of the s-scarecrows?" I stammered. "Do you mean — "

I stopped when, out of the corner of my eye, I saw the scarecrow's arm move.

The straw crinkled as the arm slid up.

Then I felt rough straw brush against my face — as the dry scarecrow arm moved to my throat.

4

The prickly straw, poking out of the sleeve of the black coat, scraped against my neck.

I let out a shrill scream.

"It's *alive!*" I cried in panic, diving to the ground, scrambling away on all fours.

I turned back to see Mark and Stanley calmly watching me.

Hadn't they seen the scarecrow try to choke me?

Then Stanley's son, Sticks, stepped out from behind the scarecrow, a gleeful grin on his face.

"Sticks — ! You creep!" I cried angrily. I knew at once that he had moved the scarecrow's arm.

"You city kids sure scare easy," Sticks said, his grin growing wider. He reached down to help me to my feet. "You really thought the scarecrow moved, didn't you, Jodie!" he said accusingly.

"I can make the scarecrows move," Stanley said, pulling the cap down lower on his forehead.

"I can make them walk. I did it. It's all in the book."

Sticks's smile faded. The light seemed to dim from his dark eyes. "Yeah, sure, Dad," he murmured.

Sticks is sixteen. He is tall and lanky. He has long, skinny arms and legs. That's how he got the nickname Sticks.

He tries to look tough. He has long black hair down past his collar, which he seldom washes. He wears tight muscle shirts and dirty jeans, ripped at the knees. He sneers a lot, and his dark eyes always seem to be laughing at you.

He calls Mark and me "the city kids." He always says it with a sneer. And he's always playing stupid jokes on us. I think he's kind of jealous of Mark and me. I don't think it's been easy for Sticks to grow up on the farm, living in the little guest house with his dad.

I mean, Stanley is more like a kid than a father.

"I saw you back there," Mark told Sticks.

"Well, thanks for warning me!" I snapped at Mark. I turned back angrily to Sticks. "I see you haven't changed at all."

"Great to see you, too, Jodie," he replied sarcastically. "The city kids are back for another month with the hicks!"

"Sticks — what's your problem?" I shot back.

"Be nice," Stanley muttered. "The corn has ears, you know."

18

We all stared at Stanley. Had he just made a joke? It was hard to tell with him.

Stanley's face remained serious. His big eyes stared out at me through the shade of his cap. "The corn has ears," he repeated. "There are spirits in the field."

Sticks shook his head unhappily. "Dad, you spend too much time with that superstition book," he muttered.

"The book is all true," Stanley replied. "It's all true."

Sticks kicked at the dirt. He raised his eyes to me. His expression seemed very sad. "Things are different here," he murmured.

"Huh?" I didn't understand. "What do you mean?"

Sticks turned to his father. Stanley was staring back at him, his eyes narrowed.

Sticks shrugged and didn't reply. He grabbed Mark's arm and squeezed it. "You're as flabby as ever," he told Mark. "Want to throw a football around this afternoon?"

"It's kind of hot," Mark replied. He wiped the sweat off his forehead with the back of his hand.

Sticks sneered at him. "Still a wimp, huh?"

"No way!" Mark protested. "I just said it was hot, that's all."

"Hey — you've got something on your back," Sticks told Mark. "Turn around."

Mark obediently turned around.

19

Sticks quickly bent down, picked up the wormy corncob, and stuffed it down the back of Mark's T-shirt.

I had to laugh as I watched my brother run screaming all the way back to the farmhouse.

Dinner was quiet. Grandma Miriam's fried chicken was as tasty as ever. And she was right about the corn. It was very sweet. Mark and I each ate two ears, dripping with butter.

I enjoyed the dinner. But it upset me that both of my grandparents seemed so changed. Grandpa Kurt used to talk nonstop. He always had dozens of funny stories about the farmers in the area. And he always had new jokes to tell.

Tonight he barely said a word.

Grandma Miriam kept urging Mark and me to eat more. And she kept asking us how we liked everything. But she, too, seemed quieter.

They both seemed tense. Uncomfortable.

They both kept glancing down the table at Stanley, who was eating with both hands, butter dripping down his chin.

Sticks sat glumly across from his father. He seemed even more unfriendly than usual.

Stanley was the only cheerful person at the table. He chewed his chicken enthusiastically and asked for a third helping of mashed potatoes.

"Is everything okay, Stanley?" Grandma Miriam kept asking, biting her bottom lip. "Everything okay?"

Stanley burped and smiled. "Not bad," was his reply.

Why do things seem so different? I wondered. Is it just because Grandma and Grandpa are getting old?

After dinner, we sat around the big, comfortable living room. Grandpa Kurt rocked gently back and forth in the antique wooden rocking chair by the fireplace.

It was too hot to build a fire. But as he rocked, he stared into the dark fireplace, a thoughtful expression on his white-stubbled face.

Grandma Miriam sat in her favorite chair, a big, green overstuffed armchair across from Grandpa Kurt. She had an unopened gardening magazine in her lap.

Sticks, who had barely said two words the whole evening, disappeared. Stanley leaned against the wall, poking his teeth with a toothpick.

Mark sank down into the long, green couch. I sat down at the other end of it and stared across the room.

"Yuck. That stuffed bear still gives me the creeps!" I exclaimed.

At the far end of the room, an enormous stuffed brown bear — about eight feet tall — stood straight up on its hind legs. Grandpa Kurt had shot it many years ago on a hunting trip. The bear's huge paws were extended, as if ready to pounce.

"That was a killer bear," Grandpa Kurt remembered, rocking slowly, his eyes on the angry-looking beast. "He mauled two hunters before I shot him. I saved their lives."

I shuddered and turned away from the bear. I really hated it. I don't know why Grandma Miriam let Grandpa Kurt keep it in the living room!

"How about a scary story?" I asked Grandpa Kurt.

He stared back at me, his blue eyes suddenly lifeless and dull.

"Yeah. We've been looking forward to your stories," Mark chimed in. "Tell us the one about the headless boy in the closet."

"No. Tell a new one," I insisted eagerly.

Grandpa Kurt rubbed his chin slowly. His eyes went to Stanley across the room. Then he cleared his throat nervously.

"I'm kind of tired, kids," he said softly. "Think I'll just go to bed."

"But — no story?" I protested.

He stared back at me with those dull eyes. "I don't really know any stories," he murmured. He slowly climbed to his feet and headed toward his room.

What is going on here? I asked myself. *What is wrong?*

5

Upstairs in my bedroom later that night, I changed into a long nightshirt. The bedroom window was open, and a soft breeze invaded the room.

I stared out the open window. A broad apple tree cast its shadow over the lawn.

Where the grass ended, the cornfields stretched out under the glow of the full moon. The pale moonlight made the tall stalks shimmer like gold. The stalks cast long blue shadows over the field.

Across the wide field, the scarecrows poked up stiffly like dark-uniformed soldiers. Their coat sleeves ruffled in the light breeze. Their pale burlap faces seemed to stare back at me.

I felt a cold chill run down my back.

So many scarecrows. At least a dozen of them, standing in straight rows. Like an army ready to march.

"The scarecrow walks at midnight."

That's what Stanley had said in that low, frightening tone I had never heard him use before.

I glanced at the clock on the bed table. Just past ten o'clock.

I'll be asleep by the time they walk, I thought. A crazy thought.

I sneezed. It seems I'm allergic to the farm air both day *and* night!

I stared at the long shadows cast by the scarecrows. A gust of wind bent the stalks, making the shadows roll forward like a dark ocean wave.

And then I saw the scarecrows start to twitch.

"Mark!" I screamed. "Mark — come here! Hurry!"

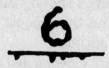

6

Under the light of the full moon, I stared in horror as the dark scarecrows started to move.

Their arms jerked. Their burlap heads lurched forward.

All of them. In unison.

All of the scarecrows were jerking, twitching, straining — as if struggling to pull free of their stakes.

"Mark — hurry!" I screamed.

I heard footsteps clomping rapidly down the hall. Mark burst breathlessly into my room. "Jodie — what *is* it?" he cried.

I motioned frantically for him to come to the window. As he stepped beside me, I pointed to the cornfields. "Look — the scarecrows."

He gripped the windowsill and leaned out the window.

Over his shoulder, I could see the scarecrows twitch in unison. A cold shudder made me wrap my arms around myself.

"It's the wind," Mark said, stepping back from the window. "What's your problem, Jodie? It's just the wind blowing them around."

"You — you're wrong, Mark," I stammered, still hugging myself. "Look again."

He rolled his eyes and sighed. But he turned back and leaned out the window. He gazed out at the field for a long time.

"Don't you see?" I demanded shrilly. "They're all moving together. Their arms, their heads — all moving together."

When Mark pulled back from the window, his blue eyes were wide and fearful. He stared at me thoughtfully and didn't say a word.

Finally, he swallowed hard and his voice came out low and frightened. "We've got to tell Grandpa Kurt," he said.

We rushed downstairs, but our grandparents had gone to bed. The bedroom door was closed. It was silent on the other side.

"Maybe we'd better wait till tomorrow morning," I whispered as Mark and I tiptoed back upstairs to our rooms. "I think we'll be safe till then."

We crept back to our rooms. I pushed the window shut and locked it. Out in the fields, the scarecrows were still twitching, still pulling at their stakes.

With a shudder, I turned away from the window

and plunged into the bed, pulling the old quilt up over my head.

I slept restlessly, tossing under the heavy quilt. In the morning, I jumped eagerly from bed. I ran a brush through my hair and hurried down to breakfast.

Mark was right behind me on the stairs. He was wearing the same jeans as yesterday and a red-and-black Nirvana T-shirt. He hadn't bothered to brush his hair. It stood straight up in back.

"Pancakes!" he managed to choke out. Mark is only good for one word at a time this early in the morning.

But the word instantly cheered me up and made me forget for a moment about the creepy scarecrows.

How could I have forgotten about Grandma Miriam's amazing chocolate chip pancakes?

They are so soft, they really do melt in your mouth. And the warm chocolate mixed with the sweet maple syrup makes the most delicious breakfast I've ever eaten.

As we hurried across the living room toward the kitchen, I sniffed the air, hoping to smell that wonderful aroma of pancake batter on the stove.

But my nose was too stuffed up to smell anything.

Mark and I burst into the kitchen at the same time. Grandpa Kurt and Stanley were already at the table. A big blue pot of coffee stood steaming in front of them.

Stanley sipped his coffee. Grandpa Kurt had his face buried behind the morning newspaper. He glanced up and smiled as Mark and I entered.

Everyone said good morning to everyone.

Mark and I took our places at the table. We were so eager for the famous pancakes, we were practically rubbing our hands together the way cartoon characters do.

Imagine our shock when Grandma Miriam set down big bowls of cornflakes in front of us.

I practically burst into tears.

I glanced across the table at Mark. He was staring back at me, his face revealing his surprise — and disappointment. "Cornflakes?" he asked in a high-pitched voice.

Grandma Miriam had gone back to the sink. I turned to her. "Grandma Miriam — no pancakes?" I asked meekly.

I saw her glance at Stanley. "I've stopped making them, Jodie," she replied, her eyes still on Stanley. "Pancakes are too fattening."

"Nothing like a good bowl of cornflakes in the morning," Stanley said with a big smile. He reached for the cornflakes box in the center of the table and filled his bowl up with a second helping.

Grandpa Kurt grunted behind his newspaper.

"Go ahead — eat them before they get soggy," Grandma Miriam urged from the sink.

Mark and I just stared at each other. Last summer, Grandma Miriam had made us a big stack of chocolate chip pancakes almost every morning!

What is going on here? I wondered once again.

I suddenly remembered Sticks out in the cornfields the day before, whispering to me, "Things are different here."

They sure were different. And not for the better, I decided.

My stomach grumbled. I picked up the spoon and started to eat my cornflakes. I saw Mark glumly spooning his. And then I suddenly remembered the twitching scarecrows.

"Grandpa Kurt — " I started. "Last night, Mark and I — we were looking out at the cornfields and we saw the scarecrows. They were moving. We — "

I heard Grandma Miriam utter a low gasp from behind me.

Grandpa Kurt lowered his newspaper. He narrowed his eyes at me, but didn't say a word.

"The scarecrows were moving!" Mark chimed in.

Stanley chuckled. "It was the wind," he said, his eyes on Grandpa Kurt. "It had to be the wind blowing them around."

Grandpa Kurt glared at Stanley. "You sure?" he demanded.

"Yeah. It was the wind," Stanley replied tensely.

"But they were trying to get off their poles!" I cried. "We *saw* them!"

Grandpa Kurt stared hard at Stanley.

Stanley's ears turned bright red. He lowered his eyes. "It was a breezy night," he said. "They move in the wind."

"It's going to be a sunny day," Grandma Miriam said brightly from the sink.

"But the scarecrows — " Mark insisted.

"Yep. Looks like a real pretty day," Grandpa Kurt mumbled, ignoring Mark.

He doesn't want to talk about the scarecrows, I realized.

Is it because he doesn't believe us?

Grandpa Kurt turned to Stanley. "After you take the cows to pasture, maybe you and Jodie and Mark can do some fishing at the creek."

"Maybe," Stanley replied, studying the cornflakes box. "Maybe we could just do that."

"Sounds like fun," Mark said. Mark likes fishing. It's one of his favorite sports because you don't have to move too much.

There's a really pretty creek behind the cow pasture at the far end of Grandpa Kurt's property. It's very woodsy back there, and the narrow creek trickles softly beneath the old shade trees and is usually filled with fish.

Finishing my cereal, I turned to Grandma Miriam at the sink. "And what are you doing today?"

I asked her. "Maybe you and I could spend some time together and — "

I stopped as she turned toward me and her hand came into view.

"Ohhhh." I let out a frightened moan when I saw her hand. It — it was made of *straw*!!

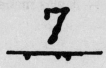

7

"Jodie — what's the matter?" Grandma Miriam asked.

I started to point to her hand.

Then it came into sharp focus, and I saw that her hand wasn't straw — she was holding a broom.

She had gripped it by the handle and was pulling lint off the ends of the straw.

"Nothing's wrong," I told her, feeling like a total jerk. I rubbed my eyes. "I've got to take my allergy medicine," I told her. "My eyes are so watery. I keep *seeing* things!"

I was seeing scarecrows everywhere I looked! I scolded myself for acting so crazy.

Stop thinking about scarecrows, I told myself. Stanley was right. The scarecrows had moved in the wind last night.

It was just the wind.

*   *   *

Stanley took us fishing later that morning. As we started off for the creek, he seemed in a really cheerful mood.

He smiled as he swung the big picnic basket Grandma Miriam had packed for our lunch. "She put in all my favorites," Stanley said happily.

He patted the basket with childish satisfaction.

He had three bamboo fishing poles tucked under his left arm. He carried the big straw basket in his right hand. He refused to let Mark and me carry anything.

The warm air smelled sweet. The sun beamed down in a cloudless, blue sky. Blades of recently cut grass stuck to my white sneakers as we headed across the back yard.

The medicine had helped. My eyes were much better.

Stanley turned just past the barn and began walking quickly along its back wall. His expression turned solemn. He appeared to be concentrating hard on something.

"Hey — where are we going?" I called, hurrying to keep up with him.

He didn't seem to hear me. Taking long strides, swinging the straw picnic basket as he walked, he headed back in the direction we started from.

"Hey — wait up!" Mark called breathlessly. My brother hates to hurry when he can take his time.

"Stanley — wait!" I cried, tugging his shirt-sleeve. "We're going around in circles!"

He nodded, his expression serious under the black baseball cap. "We have to circle the barn three times," he said in a low voice.

"Huh? Why?" I demanded.

We started our second turn around the barn.

"It will bring us good luck with our fishing," Stanley replied. Then he added, "It's in the book. Everything is in the book."

I opened my mouth to tell him this was really silly. But I decided not to. He seemed so serious about that superstition book of his. I didn't want to spoil it for him.

Besides, Mark and I could use the exercise.

A short while later, we finished circling and started walking along the dirt path that led past the cornfields to the creek. Stanley's smile returned immediately.

He really believes the superstitions in the book, I realized.

I wondered if Sticks believed them, too.

"Where's Sticks?" I asked, kicking a big clump of dirt across the path.

"Doing chores," Stanley replied. "Sticks is a good worker. A real good worker. But he'll be along soon, I bet. Sticks never likes to miss out on a fishing trip."

The sun began to feel really strong on my face

and on my shoulders. I wondered if I should run back and get some sunblock.

The dark-suited scarecrows appeared to stare at me as we walked past the tall rows of cornstalks. I could swear their pale, painted faces turned to follow me as I went by.

And did one of them lift its arm to wave a straw hand at me?

I scolded myself for such stupid thoughts, and turned my eyes away.

Stop thinking about scarecrows, Jodie! I told myself.

Forget your bad dream. Forget about the dumb scarecrows.

It's a beautiful day, and you have nothing to worry about. Try to relax and have a good time.

The path led into tall pine woods behind the cornfields. It got shady and much cooler as soon as we stepped into the woods.

"Can't we take a taxi the rest of the way?" Mark whined. A typical Mark joke. He really *would* take a taxi if there was one!

Stanley shook his head. "City kids," he muttered, grinning.

The path ended, and we continued through the trees. It smelled so piney and fresh in the woods. I saw a tiny, brown-and-white chipmunk dart into a hollow log.

In the near distance I could hear the musical trickle of the creek.

Suddenly, Stanley stopped. He bent and picked up a pinecone.

The three fishing poles fell to the ground. He didn't seem to notice. He held the pinecone close to his face, studying it.

"A pinecone on the shady side means a long winter," he said, turning the dry cone in his hand.

Mark and I bent to pick up the poles. "Is that what the book says?" Mark asked.

Stanley nodded. He set the pinecone down carefully where he found it.

"The cone is still sticky. That's a good sign," he said seriously.

Mark let out a giggle. I knew he was trying not to laugh at Stanley. But the giggle escaped somehow.

Stanley's big brown eyes filled with hurt. "It's all true, Mark," he said quietly. "It's all true."

"I — I'd like to read that book," Mark said, glancing at me.

"It's a very hard book," Stanley replied. "I have trouble with some of the words."

"I can hear the creek," I broke in, changing the subject. "Let's go. I want to catch some fish before lunchtime."

The clear water felt cold against my legs. The smooth rocks of the creek bed were slippery under my bare feet.

All three of us had waded into the shallow creek. Mark had wanted to lie down on the grassy shore to fish. But I convinced him it was much more fun — and much easier to catch something — if you stand in the water.

"Yeah, I'll catch something," he grumbled as he rolled up the cuffs of his jeans. "I'll catch pneumonia!"

Stanley let out a loud laugh. It sounded like, "Har! Har! Har!"

He set the big picnic basket down carefully on the dry grass. Then he rolled up the legs of his denim overalls. Carrying a pole high in one hand, he stepped into the water.

"Ooooh! It's cold!" he cried, waving his arms above his head, nearly losing his balance on the slippery rocks.

"Stanley — didn't you forget something?" I called to him.

He turned, confused. His big ears became bright red. "What did I forget, Jodie?"

I pointed to his fishing pole. "How about some bait?" I called.

He glanced at the empty hook on the end of his line. Then he made his way back to shore to get a worm to bait his hook.

A few minutes later, all three of us were in the water. Mark complained at first about how cold it was and about how the rocks on the bottom hurt his delicate little feet.

But after a while, he got into it, too.

The creek at this point was only about two feet deep. The water was very clear and trickled rapidly, making little swirls and dips over the rocky bottom.

I lowered my line into the water and watched the red plastic float bob on the surface. If it started to sink, I'd know I had a bite.

The sun felt warm on my face. The cool water flowed past pleasantly.

I wish it were deep enough to swim here, I thought.

"Hey — I've got something!" Mark cried excitedly.

Stanley and I turned and watched him tug up his line.

Mark pulled with all his might. "It — it's a big one, I think," he said.

Finally, he gave one last really hard tug — and pulled up a thick clump of green weeds.

"Good one, Mark," I said, rolling my eyes. "It's a big one, all right."

"*You're* a big one," Mark shot back. "A big jerk."

"Don't be such a baby," I muttered.

I brushed away a buzzing horsefly and tried to concentrate on my line. But my mind started to wander. It always does when I'm fishing.

I found myself thinking about the tall scarecrows in the field. They stood so darkly, so menacingly, so alert. Their painted faces all had the same hard stare.

I was still picturing them when I felt the hand slip around my ankle.

The straw scarecrow hand.

It reached up from the water, circled my ankle, and started to tighten its cold, wet grip around my leg.

I screamed and tried to kick the hand away.

But my feet slipped on the smooth rocks. My hands shot up as I toppled backwards.

"Ohh!" I cried out again as I hit the water.

The scarecrow hung on.

On my back, the water rushing over me, I kicked and thrashed my arms.

And then I saw it. The clump of green weeds that had wrapped itself around my ankle.

"Oh, no," I moaned out loud.

No scarecrow. Only weeds.

I lowered my foot to the water. I didn't move. I just lay there on my back, waiting for my heart to stop pounding, feeling once again like a total jerk.

I glanced up at Mark and Stanley. They were staring down at me, too startled to laugh.

"Don't say a word," I warned them, struggling to my feet. "I'm warning you — don't say a word."

Mark snickered, but he obediently didn't say anything.

"I didn't bring a towel," Stanley said with concern. "I'm sorry, Jodie, I didn't know you wanted to swim."

That made Mark burst out in loud guffaws.

I shot Mark a warning stare. My T-shirt and shorts were soaked. I started to shore, carrying the pole awkwardly in front of me.

"I don't need a towel," I told Stanley. "It feels good. Very refreshing."

"You scared away all the fish, Jodie," Mark complained.

"No. *You* scared them away. They saw your *face!*" I replied. I knew I was acting like a baby now. But I didn't care. I was cold and wet and angry.

I stomped onto the shore, shaking water from my hair.

"I think they're biting better down here," I heard Stanley call to Mark. I turned to see him disappear around a curve of the creek.

Stepping carefully over the rocks, Mark followed after him. They were both hidden from view behind the thick trees.

I squeezed my hair, trying to get the creek water out. Finally, I gave up and tossed my hair behind my shoulder.

I was debating what to do next when I heard a crackling sound in the woods.

41

A footstep?

I turned and stared into the trees. I didn't see anyone.

Another chipmunk scurried away over the blanket of dead, brown leaves. Had someone — or some*thing* — frightened the chipmunk?

I listened hard. Another crackling footstep. Rustling sounds.

"Who — who's there?" I called.

The low bushes rustled in reply.

"Sticks — is that you? Sticks?" My voice trembled.

No reply.

It *has* to be Sticks, I told myself. This is Grandpa Kurt's property. No one else would be back here.

"Sticks — stop trying to scare me!" I shouted angrily.

No reply.

Another footstep. The crack of a twig.

More rustling sounds. Closer now.

"Sticks — I know it's you!" I called uncertainly. "I'm really tired of your dumb tricks. Sticks?"

My eyes stared straight ahead into the trees.

I listened. Silence now.

Heavy silence.

And then I raised my hand to my mouth as I saw the dark figure poke out from the shade of two tall pines.

"Sticks — ?"

I squinted into the deep blue shadows.

I saw the bulging, dark coat. The faded burlap head. The dark fedora hat tilted over the black, painted eyes.

I saw the straw poking out under the jacket. The straw sticking out from the long jacket sleeves.

A scarecrow.

A scarecrow that had followed us? Followed us to the creek?

Squinting hard into the shadows, staring at its evil, frozen grin, I opened my mouth to scream — but no sound came out.

9

And then a hand grabbed my shoulder.

"Ohh!" I let out a cry and spun around.

Stanley stared at me with concern. He and Mark had come up behind me.

"Jodie, what's the matter?" Stanley asked. "Mark and I — we thought we heard you calling."

"What's up?" Mark asked casually. The line on his fishing pole had become tangled, and he was working to untangle it. "Did you see a squirrel or something?"

"No — I — I — " My heart was pounding so hard, I could barely speak.

"Cool your jets, Jodie," Mark said, imitating me.

"I saw a scarecrow!" I finally managed to scream.

Stanley's mouth dropped open.

Mark narrowed his eyes suspiciously at me. "A scarecrow? Here in the woods?"

44

"It — it was walking," I stammered. "I heard it. I heard it walking."

A choking sound escaped Stanley's open mouth.

Mark continued to stare at me, his features tight with fear.

"It's over there!" I cried. "Right there! Look!" I pointed.

But it was gone.

10

Stanley stared hard at me, his big brown eyes filled with confusion.

"I saw it," I insisted. "Between those two trees." I pointed again.

"You did? A scarecrow? Really?" Stanley asked. I could see he was really starting to get scared.

"Well . . . maybe it was just the shadows," I said. I didn't want to frighten Stanley.

I shivered. "I'm soaked. I've got to get back in the sunlight," I told them.

"But did you see it?" Stanley asked, his big eyes locked on mine. "Did you see a scarecrow here, Jodie?"

"I — I don't think so, Stanley," I replied, trying to calm him down. "I'm sorry."

"This is very bad," he murmured, talking to himself. "This is very bad. I have to read the book. This is very bad." Then, muttering to himself, he turned and ran.

46

"Stanley — stop!" I called. "Stanley — come back! Don't leave us down here!"

But he was gone. Vanished into the woods.

"I'm going after him," I told Mark. "And then I'm going to tell Grandpa Kurt about this. Can you carry back the fishing poles by yourself?"

"Do I have to?" Mark whined. My brother is so lazy!

I told him he had to. Then I went running along the path through the woods toward the farmhouse.

My heart pounded as I reached the cornfields. The dark-coated scarecrows appeared to stare at me. As my sneakers thudded on the narrow dirt path, I imagined the straw arms reaching for me, reaching to grab me and pull me into the corn.

But the scarecrows kept their silent, still watch over the cornstalks. They didn't move or twitch as I hurtled past.

Up ahead I saw Stanley running to his little house. I cupped my hands over my mouth and called to him, but he disappeared inside.

I decided to find Grandpa Kurt and tell him about the scarecrow I saw moving through the woods.

The barn door was open, and I thought I saw someone moving around inside. "Grandpa Kurt?" I called breathlessly. "Are you in there?"

My wet hair bounced on my shoulders as I ran

into the barn. I stood in the rectangle of light that stretched from the doorway and stared into the darkness. "Grandpa Kurt?" I called, struggling to catch my breath.

My eyes slowly adjusted to the dim light. I stepped deeper into the barn. "Grandpa Kurt? Are you here?"

Hearing a soft scraping sound against the far wall, I made my way toward it. "Grandpa Kurt — can I talk to you? I really need to talk to you!" My voice sounded tiny and frightened in the big, dark barn. My sneakers scraped over the dry straw floor as I walked toward the back.

I spun around as I heard a rumbling sound.

The light grew dimmer.

"Hey — " I shouted. Too late.

The barn door was sliding shut.

"Hey! Who's there?" I cried out in stunned anger. "Hey — stop!"

I slipped over the straw as I started to lurch toward the sliding door. I fell down hard, but quickly scrambled to my feet.

I darted toward the door. But I wasn't fast enough.

As the heavy door rumbled shut, the rectangle of light grew narrower, narrower.

The door slammed with a deafening *bang*.

The darkness slid around me, circled me, covered me.

"Hey — let me out!" I screamed. "Let me out of here!"

My scream ended in a choked sob. My breath escaped in noisy gasps.

I pounded on the wooden barn door with both fists. Then I frantically swept my hands over the door, searching blindly for a latch, for something to pull — some way to open the door.

When I couldn't find anything, I pounded on the door until my fists hurt.

Then I stopped and took a step back.

Calm down, Jodie, I told myself. Calm down. You'll get out of the barn. You'll find a way out. It's not like you're trapped in here forever.

I tried to force away my panic. I held my breath, waiting for my heart to stop racing. Then I let my breath out slowly. Slooooowly.

I was just starting to feel a little better when I heard the scraping sound.

A dry scraping. The sound of a shoe crunching over straw.

"Oh." I let out a sharp cry, then raised both hands to my face and listened.

Scrape. Scrape. Scrape.

The sound of footsteps. Slow, steady footsteps, so light on the barn floor.

Footsteps coming toward me in the darkness.

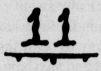

11

"Who — who's there?" I choked out, my voice a hushed whisper.

No reply.

Scrape. Scrape. Scrape.

The soft, scratchy footsteps came closer.

"Who *is* it?" I cried shrilly.

No reply.

I stared into the darkness. I couldn't see a thing.

Scrape. Scrape.

Whoever — or whatever — was moving steadily toward me.

I took a step back. Then another.

I tried to cry out, but my throat was choked with fear.

I let out a terrified gasp as I backed into something. In my panic, it took me a few seconds to realize that it was only a wooden ladder. The ladder that led up to the hayloft.

The footsteps crunched closer. Closer.

"Please — " I uttered in a tiny, choked voice. "Please — don't — "

Closer. Closer. Scraping toward me through the heavy darkness.

I gripped the sides of the ladder. "Please — leave me alone!"

Before I realized what I was doing, I was pulling myself up the ladder. My arms trembled, and my legs felt as if they each weighed a thousand pounds.

But I scrambled rung by rung toward the hayloft, away from the frightening, scraping footsteps down below.

When I reached the top, I lay flat on the hayloft floor. I struggled to listen, to hear the footsteps over the loud pounding of my heart.

Was I being followed? Was the thing chasing me up the ladder?

I held my breath. I listened.

Scrabbling sounds. Scraping footsteps.

"Go away!" I screamed frantically. "Whoever you are — go away!"

But the sounds continued, dry and scratchy. Like straw brushing against straw.

Scrambling to my knees, I turned to the small, square hayloft window. Sunlight filtered in through the window. The light made the hay strewn over the floor gleam like slender strands of gold.

My heart still pounding, I crawled to the window.

Yes! The heavy rope was still tied to the side. The rope that Mark and I always used to swing down to the ground.

I can get out of here! I told myself happily.

I can grab the rope and swing out of the hayloft. I can escape!

Eagerly, I grabbed the rope with both hands.

Then I poked my head out the window and gazed down to the ground.

And let out a scream of surprise and horror.

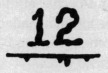

12

Gazing down, I saw a black hat. Beneath it, a black coat.

A scarecrow. Perched outside the barn door. As if standing guard.

It jerked its arms and legs at the sound of my scream.

And as I stared in disbelief, it hurried around the side of the barn, hobbling on its straw legs, its arms flapping at its sides.

I blinked several times.

Was I *seeing* things?

My hands were cold and wet. I gripped the rope more tightly. Taking a deep breath, I plunged out of the small square window.

The heavy rope swung out over the front of the barn.

Down, down. I hit the ground hard, landing on my feet.

"Ow!" I cried out as the rope cut my hands.

I let go and ran around to the side of the barn.

I wanted to catch up to that scarecrow. I wanted to see if it really was a scarecrow, a scarecrow that could run.

Ignoring my fear, I ran as fast as I could.

No sign of him on this side of the barn.

My chest began to ache. My temples throbbed.

I turned the corner and headed around the back of the barn, searching for the fleeing scarecrow.

And ran right into Sticks!

"Hey — " We both shouted in surprise as we collided.

I frantically untangled myself from him. Staring past him, I saw that the scarecrow had vanished.

"What's the hurry?" Sticks demanded. "You practically ran me over!"

He was wearing faded denim jeans, slashed at both knees, and a faded purple muscle shirt that only showed off how skinny he was. His black hair was tied back in a short ponytail.

"A — a scarecrow!" I stammered.

And, then — that instant — I knew.

In that instant, I solved the whole mystery of the scarecrows.

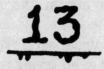

13

It hadn't been a scarecrow.

It was Sticks.

In the woods down by the creek. And, now, outside the barn.

Sticks. Playing another one of his mean tricks.

And I was suddenly certain that Sticks had somehow made the scarecrows twitch and pull on their stakes last night.

Sticks just loved fooling the "city kids." Ever since Mark and I had been little, he'd played the scariest, meanest practical jokes on us.

Sometimes Sticks could be a nice guy. But he had a real cruel streak.

"I thought you were fishing," he said casually.

"Well, I'm not," I snapped. "Sticks, why do you keep trying to scare us?"

"Huh?" He pretended he didn't know what I was talking about.

"Sticks, give me a break," I muttered. "I know you were the scarecrow just now. I'm not stupid!"

"Scarecrow? What scarecrow?" he asked, giving me a wide-eyed, innocent expression.

"You were dressed as a scarecrow," I accused him. "Or else you carried one here, and pulled it on a string or something."

"You're totally crazy," Sticks replied angrily. "Have you been out in the sun too long or something?"

"Sticks — give up," I said. "Why are you doing this? Why do you keep trying to scare Mark and me? You scared your Dad, too."

"Jodie, you're nuts!" he exclaimed. "I really don't have time to be dressing up in costumes just to amuse you and your brother."

"Sticks — you're not fooling me," I insisted. "You — "

I stopped short when I saw Sticks's expression change. "Dad!" he cried, suddenly frightened. "Dad! You say he was scared?"

I nodded.

"I've got to find him!" Sticks exclaimed frantically, "He — he could do something *terrible*!"

"Sticks, your joke has gone far enough!" I cried. "Just *stop* it!"

But he was already running toward the front of the barn, calling for his father, his voice shrill and frantic.

Sticks didn't find his dad until dinnertime. That's the next time I saw him, too — just before

56

dinner. He was carrying his big superstition book, holding it tightly under his arm.

"Jodie," he whispered, motioning for me to come close. His face was red. His dark eyes revealed his excitement.

"Hi, Stanley," I whispered back uncertainly.

"Don't tell Grandpa Kurt about the scarecrow," Stanley whispered.

"Huh?" Stanley's request caught me off guard.

"Don't tell your grandpa," Stanley repeated. "It will only upset him. We don't want to frighten him, do we?"

"But, Stanley — " I started to protest.

Stanley raised a finger to his lips. "Don't tell, Jodie. Your grandpa doesn't like to be upset. I'll take care of the scarecrow. I have the book." He tapped the big book with his finger.

I started to tell Stanley that the scarecrow was only Sticks, playing a mean joke. But Grandma Miriam called us to the table before I could get the words out.

Stanley carried his superstition book to the table. Every few bites, he would pick up the big, black book and read a few paragraphs.

He moved his lips as he read. But I was sitting down at the other end of the table and couldn't make out any of the words.

Sticks kept his eyes down on his plate and hardly said a word. I think he was really embarrassed that his father was reading the superstition book at the dinner table.

But Grandpa Kurt and Grandma Miriam didn't act the least bit surprised. They talked cheerfully to Mark and me and kept passing us more food — as if they didn't even notice Stanley's behavior.

I really wanted to tell Grandpa Kurt about how Sticks was trying to scare Mark and me. But I decided to listen to Stanley and not upset my grandfather.

Besides, I could deal with Sticks if I had to. He thought he was so tough. But I wasn't the least bit afraid of him.

Stanley was still reading, jabbering away as he read, as Grandma Miriam cleared the dinner dishes. Mark and I helped. Then we took our seats as Grandma Miriam carried a big cherry pie to the table.

"Weird," Mark whispered to me, staring at the pie.

He was right. "Doesn't Grandpa Kurt like *apple* pie?" I blurted out.

Grandma Miriam gave me a tense smile. "Too early in the year for apples," she murmured.

"But isn't Grandpa Kurt allergic to cherries?" Mark asked.

Grandma Miriam started cutting the pie with a silver pie cutter. "Everyone loves cherry pie," she replied, concentrating on her work. Then she raised her eyes to Stanley. "Isn't that right, Stanley?"

Stanley grinned over his book. "It's my favorite," he said. "Grandma Miriam always serves my favorite."

After dinner, Grandpa Kurt once again refused to tell Mark and me a scary story.

We were sitting around the fireplace, staring at the crackling yellow flames. Even though it had been so hot, the air had grown cool this evening, cool enough to build a nice, toasty fire.

Grandpa Kurt was in his rocking chair at the side of the hearth. The old wooden chair creaked as he rocked slowly back and forth.

He had always loved to gaze at the fire and tell us one of his frightening stories. You could see the leaping flames reflected in his blue eyes. And his voice would go lower and lower as the story got scarier.

But tonight he shrugged when I asked him for a story. He stared dully at the huge stuffed bear on its pedestal against the wall. Then he glanced across the room at Stanley.

"Wish I knew some good stories," Grandpa Kurt replied with a sigh. "But I've clean run out."

A short while later, Mark and I trudged upstairs to our bedrooms. "What is his problem?" Mark whispered as we climbed.

I shook my head. "Beats me."

"He seems so . . . different," Mark said.

"Everyone here does," I agreed. "Except for Sticks. He's still trying to scare us city kids."

"Let's just ignore him," Mark suggested. "Let's just pretend we don't see him running around in his stupid scarecrow costume."

I agreed. Then I said good-night and headed into my room.

Ignore the scarecrows, I thought as I arranged the blankets on the bed.

Just ignore them.

I'm not going to think about scarecrows again, I told myself.

Sticks can go jump in the creek.

Climbing into bed, I pulled the quilt up to my chin. I lay on my back, staring up at the cracks in the ceiling, trying to figure out what kind of picture they formed. There were three jagged cracks. I decided they looked like bolts of lightning.

If I squinted, I could make them look like an old man with a beard.

I yawned. I felt really sleepy, but I couldn't get to sleep.

It was only my second night here at the farm. It always takes me awhile to adjust to being in a new place and sleeping in a different bed.

I closed my eyes. Through the open window, I could hear the soft mooing of cows from the barn.

60

And I could hear the whisper of the wind as it brushed through the tall cornstalks.

My nose was totally stuffed up. Bet I snore tonight, I thought.

That is, if I ever get to sleep!

I tried counting sheep. It didn't seem to be working, so I tried counting cows. Big, bulky, bouncing, sloooooow-moooooving cows.

I counted to a hundred twelve before I decided that wasn't working, either.

I turned onto my side. Then, after a few minutes, I tried my other side.

I found myself thinking about my best friend, Shawna. I wondered if Shawna was having a good time at camp.

I thought about some of my other friends. Most of them were just hanging around this summer, not doing much of anything.

When I glanced at the clock, I was surprised to see it was nearly twelve. I've *got* to get to sleep, I told myself. I'll be *wrecked* tomorrow if I don't get some sleep.

I settled onto my back, pulling the soft quilt up to my chin again. I closed my eyes and tried to picture nothing. Just empty, black space. Endless, empty space.

The next thing I knew, I was hearing scratching sounds.

I ignored them at first. I thought the curtains were flapping against the open window.

Got to get to sleep, I urged myself. *Got to get to sleep*.

The scratching grew louder. Closer.

I heard a scraping sound.

From outside the window?

I opened my eyes. Shadows danced on the ceiling. I realized I was holding my breath.

Listening hard.

Another scrape. More scratching. Dry scratching.

I heard a low groan.

"Huh?" A startled gasp escaped my lips.

I pulled myself up against the headboard. I tugged the quilt up to my chin, gripping it tightly with both hands.

I heard more dry scraping. Like sandpaper, I thought.

Suddenly the room grew darker.

I saw something pull itself up to the window. A dark figure. Blocking the moonlight.

"Who — who's there?" I tried to call. But my voice came out a choked whisper.

I could see a shadowy head, black against the purple sky.

It rose up in the window. Dark shoulders. Followed by a darker chest. Black against black.

A silent shadow, slipping into my room.

"H-help!" Another stammered whisper.

My heart had stopped beating. I couldn't breathe. Couldn't breathe.

It slid over the windowsill. Brushed away the curtains as it lowered itself into my room.

Its feet scraped over the bare floorboards.

Scratch scratch scratch.

It moved slowly, steadily toward my bed.

I struggled to get up.

Too late.

My feet tangled in the quilt.

I fell to the floor, landing hard on my elbows.

I raised my eyes to see it move closer.

I opened my mouth to scream as it emerged from the shadows.

And then I recognized him. Recognized his face.

"Grandpa Kurt!" I cried. "Grandpa Kurt — what are you doing here? Why did you climb in the window?"

He didn't reply. His cold blue eyes glared down at me. His whole face twisted into an ugly frown.

And then he raised both arms above me.

And I saw that he had no hands.

Clumps of straw poked out from his jacket sleeves.

Only straw.

"Grandpa — *no!!*" I shrieked.

14

"Grandpa — *please* — *no!*" I shrieked as he lowered his straw arms toward me.

He bared his teeth like an angry dog and let out a sharp, frightening growl.

The straw hands reached down for me.

Grandpa Kurt's face was the same. The face I had always known. Except that his eyes were so cold, so cold and dead.

The straw hands brushed over my face as I climbed to my feet. I took a step back, raising my hands like a shield.

"Grandpa — what's wrong? What's happening?" I whispered.

My temples were pounding. My entire body shook.

His cold eyes narrowed in fury as he reached for me again.

"Noooo!" I let out a long wail of terror. Then I turned and stumbled to the door.

His feet scraped over the bare floor as he

lurched toward me. Glancing down, I saw the straw poking out from the cuffs of his pants.

His feet — they were straw, too.

"Grandpa Kurt! Grandpa Kurt! What is *happening*?" Was that really my voice, so shrill and frightened?

He swung an arm. The straw scratched my back as it swept over me.

I grabbed for the doorknob. Twisted it. Pulled open the door.

And cried out again as I collided with Grandma Miriam.

"Oh, help! Please help! Grandma Miriam — he's *chasing* me!" I cried.

Her expression didn't change. She stared back at me.

In the dim light of the hallway, her face came into focus.

And I saw that her glasses were *painted* on.

And her eyes. And mouth. And big round nose.

Her entire face was painted on.

"You're not real!" I cried.

And then darkness swept over me as Grandpa Kurt's straw hands wrapped around my face.

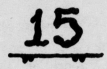

15

I woke up coughing and choking.

Surrounded by darkness. Heavy darkness.

It took me a few seconds to realize that I'd been sleeping with the pillow over my face.

Tossing it to the foot of the bed, I pulled myself up, breathing hard. My face was hot. My nightshirt stuck wetly to my back.

I glanced at the window, suddenly afraid that I'd see a dark figure climbing in.

The curtains fluttered gently. The early morning sky was still gray. I heard the shrill cry of a rooster.

A dream. It had all been a frightening nightmare.

Taking a deep breath and letting it out slowly, I lowered my feet to the floor.

I stared at the gray morning light through the window. Just a dream, I assured myself. Calm down, Jodie. It was just a dream.

I could hear someone moving around downstairs. Staggering over to the dresser, I pulled out some fresh clothes — a pair of faded denim cutoffs, a sleeveless blue T-shirt.

My eyes were watery. Everything was a blur. My allergies were really bad this morning.

Rubbing my eyes, I made my way to the window and peered out. A red ball of a sun was just peeking over the broad apple tree. A heavy morning dew made the grass of the back yard sparkle like emeralds.

The sea of cornstalks rose darkly behind the grass. The scarecrows stood stiffly over them, arms outstretched as if welcoming the morning.

The rooster crowed again.

What a stupid nightmare, I thought. I shook myself as if trying to shake it from my memory. Then I ran a brush through my hair and hurried down to breakfast.

Mark was just entering the kitchen as I came in. We found Grandma Miriam by herself at the table. A mug of tea steamed in front of her as she gazed out the window at the morning sunlight.

She turned and smiled at us as we entered. "Good morning. Sleep well?"

I was tempted to tell her about my scary nightmare. But, instead, I asked, "Where's Grandpa Kurt?" I stared at his empty chair. The newspaper lay unopened on the table.

"They all went off early," Grandma Miriam replied.

She stood up, walked to the cabinets, and brought a big box of cornflakes to the table. She motioned for us to take our places. "Pretty day," she said cheerfully.

"No pancakes?" Mark blurted out.

Grandma Miriam stopped halfway across the room. "I've completely forgotten how to make them," she said without turning around.

She set two bowls down and made her way to the refrigerator to get the milk. "You kids want orange juice this morning? It's fresh squeezed."

Grandma Miriam set the milk carton down beside my bowl. She smiled at me. Her eyes remained dull behind her square-rimmed glasses. "I hope you two are enjoying your visit," she said quietly.

"We would be if it weren't for Sticks," I blurted out.

Her expression turned to surprise. "Sticks?"

"He's trying to scare us again," I said.

Grandma Miriam tsk-tsked. "You know Sticks," she replied softly.

She pushed at her red hair with both hands. "What are you two planning for today?" she asked brightly. "It's a beautiful morning to go riding. Before they left this morning, Grandpa Kurt had Stanley saddle up Betsy and Maggie, in case you wanted to ride."

"Sounds like fun," I told her. "What do you say, Mark? Before it gets really hot out?"

"I guess," Mark replied.

"You two always enjoyed riding along the creek," Grandma Miriam said, putting the cornflakes box away.

I stared across the room at her, stared at her red, curly hair, her pudgy arms, her flowered housedress.

"Are you okay, Grandma Miriam?" I asked. The words just tumbled out of my mouth. "Is everything okay here?"

She didn't reply. Instead, she lowered her eyes, avoiding my gaze. "Go have your ride," she said quietly. "Don't worry about me."

Grandpa Kurt always called Betsy and Maggie the "old gray mares." I guess because they were both old and they were both gray. And they were as grumpy as can be when Mark and I climbed onto their saddles and started to urge them from the barn.

They were the perfect horses for us "city kids." The only time we ever got to ride horses was during our summers at the farm. So we were not exactly the most skillful riders in the world.

Bumping along on these two old nags was just our speed. And even as slow as we were moving, I dug my knees into Betsy's sides and held onto the saddle horn for dear life.

We followed the dirt path past the cornfields toward the woods. The sun was still climbing a hazy, yellow sky. But the air was already hot and sticky.

Flies buzzed around me as I bounced on top of Betsy. I removed one hand from the saddle horn to brush a big one off Betsy's back.

Several scarecrows stared back at us as Mark and I rode past. Their black eyes glared at us from under their floppy hats.

Mark and I didn't say a word. We were keeping to our promise of not talking about scarecrows.

I turned my eyes to the woods and tossed the reins, urging Betsy to move a little faster. She ignored me, of course, and kept clopping along over the path at her slow, steady pace.

"I wonder if these horses can still get up to a trot," Mark called. He was a few paces behind me on the narrow dirt path.

"Let's give it a try!" I called back, grabbing the reins tighter.

I dug my sneaker heels into Betsy's side. "Go, girl — go!" I cried, slapping her gently with the reins.

"Whoooa!" I let out a startled cry as the old horse obediently began to trot. I really didn't think she would cooperate!

"All *right*! Cool!" I heard Mark shout behind me.

Their hooves clopped loudly on the path as the two horses began to pick up speed. I was bouncing hard over the saddle, holding on tightly, off-balance, beginning to wonder if this was such a hot idea.

I didn't have a chance to cry out when the dark figure hurtled across the path.

It all happened so fast.

Betsy was trotting rapidly. I was bouncing on the saddle, bouncing so hard, my feet slipped out of the stirrups.

The dark figure leaped out right in front of us.

Betsy let out a shrill, startled whinny — and reared back.

As I started to fall, I saw immediately what had jumped onto the path.

It was a grinning scarecrow.

16

Betsy rose up with a high whinny.

My hand grabbed for the reins, but they slipped from my grasp.

The sky appeared to roll over me, then tilt away.

I slid backwards, out of the saddle, off the horse, my feet thrashing wildly for the flapping stirrups.

The sky tilted even more.

I hit the ground hard on my back.

I remember only the shock of stopping so abruptly, the surprise at how hard the ground felt, how so much pain shot through my body so quickly.

The sky turned bright red. A glowing scarlet. Like an explosion.

And then the scarlet faded to deep, deep, endlessly deep black.

*   *   *

I heard low moans before I opened my eyes.

I recognized the voice. Mark's voice.

My eyes still shut, I opened my mouth to call to him. My lips moved, but no sound came out.

"Ohhhh." Another low groan from him, not far from me.

"Mark — ?" I managed to choke out. My back ached. My shoulders hurt. My head throbbed.

Everything hurt.

"My wrist — I think I broke it," Mark said, his voice shrill and frightened.

"You fell, too?" I asked.

"Yeah. I fell, too," he groaned.

I opened my eyes. Finally. I opened my eyes. And saw the hazy sky.

All a blur. Everything was a watery blur.

I stared at the sky, trying to get it in focus.

And then saw a hand in front of the sky. A hand lowering itself toward me.

A bony hand stretching out from a heavy black coat.

The hand of the scarecrow, I realized, staring up helplessly at it.

The hand of the scarecrow, coming down to grab me.

17

The hand grabbed my shoulder.

Too terrified to cry out, too dazed to think clearly, my eyes followed the dark coat sleeve — up to the shoulder — up to the face.

A blur. All a frightening blur.

And then the face became clear.

"Stanley!" I cried.

He leaned over me, his red ears glowing, his face tight with worry. He gently grabbed my shoulder. "Jodie — are you all right?"

"Stanley — it's you!" I exclaimed happily. I sat up. "I think I'm okay. I don't know. Everything hurts."

"What a bad fall," Stanley said softly. "I was in the field. And I saw it. I saw the scarecrow. . . ."

His voice trailed off. I followed his frightened gaze up ahead of me on the dirt path.

The scarecrow lay facedown across the path.

"I saw it jump out," Stanley uttered with a shudder that shook his whole body.

"My wrist . . ." Mark moaned from nearby.

I turned as Stanley hurried over to him. Mark was sitting up in the grass at the side of the path, holding his wrist. "Look — it's starting to swell up," he groaned.

"Oooh, that's bad. That's bad," Stanley said, shaking his head.

"Maybe it's just a sprain," I suggested.

"Yeah," Stanley quickly agreed. "We'd better get you to the house and put ice on it. Can you get back up on Maggie? I'll ride behind you."

"Where's *my* horse?" I asked, searching both ways along the path. I climbed unsteadily to my feet.

"She galloped back to the barn," Stanley replied, pointing. "Fastest I've seen her go in years!"

He glanced down at the scarecrow and shuddered again.

I took a few steps, stretching my arms and my back. "I'm okay," I told him. "Take Mark on the horse. I'll walk back."

Stanley eagerly started to help Mark to his feet. I could see that Stanley wanted to get away from here — away from the scarecrow — as fast as possible.

I watched as they rode off down the path toward

the house. Stanley sat behind Mark in the saddle, holding the reins, keeping Maggie at a slow, gentle pace. Mark held his wrist against his chest and leaned back against Stanley.

I stretched my arms over my head again, trying to stretch the soreness from my back. My head ached. But other than that, I didn't feel bad.

"Guess I'm lucky," I murmured out loud.

I took a long glance at the scarecrow, sprawled facedown across the path. Cautiously, I walked over to it.

I poked its side with the toe of my sneaker.

The straw beneath the coat crinkled.

I poked it harder, pushing my sneaker hard into the scarecrow's middle.

I don't know what I expected to happen. Did I think the scarecrow would cry out? Try to squirm away?

With an angry cry, I kicked the scarecrow. Hard.

I kicked it again.

The burlap bag head bounced on the path. The scarecrow's ghastly painted grin didn't move.

It's just a scarecrow, I told myself, giving it one last kick that sent straw falling out from the jacket front.

Just a scarecrow that Sticks tossed onto the path.

Mark and I could have been killed, I told myself.
We're lucky we weren't.
Sticks. It had to be Sticks.
But why?
This wasn't a joke.
Why was Sticks trying to *hurt* us?

18

Stanley and Sticks weren't at lunch. Grandpa Kurt said they had to go into town for supplies.

Mark's wrist was only sprained. Grandma Miriam put an ice bag on it, and the swelling went right down. But Mark was groaning and complaining. He was really making the most of it.

"Guess I'll have to lie on the couch and watch TV for a week or so," he moaned.

Grandma Miriam served ham sandwiches and homemade coleslaw. Mark and I gobbled down our lunches. All that excitement had made us really hungry.

As we ate, I decided to tell Grandpa Kurt everything that had been happening. I couldn't hold it in any longer.

I told him about how Sticks was making the scarecrows move at night. And how he was trying to frighten us, trying to make us think the scarecrows were alive.

I caught a glimpse of fear in Grandpa Kurt's

blue eyes. But then he rubbed his white-stubbled cheeks, and he got a faraway look on his face.

"Sticks and his little jokes," he said finally, a smile spreading across his face. "That boy sure likes his jokes."

"He's not joking," I insisted. "He's really trying to frighten us, Grandpa."

"We could have been killed this morning!" Mark joined in. He had mayonnaise smeared on his cheek.

"Sticks is a good boy," Grandma Miriam murmured. She was smiling, too. She and Grandpa Kurt exchanged glances.

"Sticks wouldn't really hurt you," Grandpa Kurt said softly. "He just likes to have his fun."

"Great fun!" I muttered sarcastically, rolling my eyes.

"Yeah. Great fun," Mark groaned. "I almost broke my wrist!"

Grandpa Kurt and Grandma Miriam just smiled back at us, their faces frozen like the painted scarecrow faces.

After lunch, Mark slumped to the couch, where he planned to spend the rest of the afternoon staring at the TV. He *loved* having an excuse not to go outdoors.

I heard Stanley's truck pull up the drive. I decided to go find Sticks and tell him how fed up we were with his stupid scarecrow tricks.

I didn't think his jokes were all in fun. I really believed he was trying to frighten us or hurt us — and I wanted to find out why.

I didn't see Sticks or Stanley out in the yard. So I made my way across the grass to the guest house where they lived.

It was a warm, beautiful day. The sky was clear and bright. The air smelled fresh and sweet.

But I couldn't enjoy the sunshine. All I could think about was letting Sticks know how angry I was.

I knocked on the guest house door. I took a deep breath and tossed my hair behind my shoulders, listening for signs of life inside.

I tried to think of what I was going to say to Sticks. But I was too angry to plan it. My heart started to pound. I realized I was breathing hard.

I knocked on the door again, harder this time. There was no one inside.

I turned my gaze to the cornfields. The stalks stood stiffly, watched over by the motionless scarecrows. No sign of Sticks.

I turned to the barn, across the wide grass from the guest house. Maybe Sticks is in there, I thought.

I jogged to the barn. Two enormous crows hopped along the ground in front of the open barn doors. They flapped their wings hard and scrambled out of my way.

"Hey — Sticks?" I shouted breathlessly as I stepped inside.

No reply.

The barn was dark. I waited for my eyes to adjust.

Remembering my last creepy visit to the barn, I stepped reluctantly, my sneakers scraping over the straw on the floor. "Sticks? Are you in here?" I called, staring hard into the deep shadows.

A rusted baling machine stood to one side of the straw bales. A wheelbarrow tilted against the wall. I hadn't noticed them before.

"Guess he isn't here," I said to myself out loud.

I walked past the wheelbarrow. I saw something else I hadn't noticed before — a pile of old coats on the barn floor. Empty burlap bags were stacked beside them.

I picked one up. It had a frowning face painted on it in black paint. I dropped the bag back onto the pile.

These must be Stanley's scarecrow supplies, I realized.

How many more scarecrows did he plan to build?

Then something in the corner caught my eye. I walked quickly over the straw. Then I bent down to examine what I saw.

Torches. At least a dozen torches, stacked in the corner, hidden by the darkness. Next to them I spotted a large bottle of kerosene.

What on earth are *these* doing here? I asked myself.

Suddenly, I heard a scraping sound. I saw shadows slide against shadows.

And I realized that once again I was no longer alone.

I jumped to my feet. "Sticks!" I cried. "You scared me."

His face was half hidden in darkness. His black hair fell over his forehead. He didn't smile. "I warned you," he said menacingly.

19

Feeling the fear rise to my throat, I stepped out of the corner and moved past him, into the light from the doorway. "I — I was looking for you," I stammered. "Sticks, why are you trying to scare Mark and me?"

"I warned you," he said, lowering his voice to a whisper. "I warned you to get away from here, to go back home."

"But why?" I demanded. "What's your problem, Sticks? What did we do to you? Why are you trying to scare us?"

"I'm not," Sticks replied. He glanced back nervously to the barn doors.

"Huh?" I gaped at him.

"I'm not trying to scare you. Really," he insisted.

"Liar," I muttered angrily. "You must really think I'm a moron. I *know* you threw that scarecrow onto our path this morning. It had to be you, Sticks."

"I really don't know what you're talking about," he insisted coldly. "But I'm warning you — "

A sound at the doorway made him stop.

We both saw Stanley step into the barn. He shielded his eyes with one hand as his eyes adjusted to the darkness. "Sticks — are you in here?" he called.

Sticks's features tightened in sudden fear. He let out a low gasp.

"I — I've got to go," Sticks whispered tensely to me. He turned and started jogging toward Stanley. "Here I am, Dad," he called. "Is the tractor ready?"

I watched the two of them hurry from the barn. Sticks didn't look back.

I stood in the darkness, my eyes on the empty doorway, thinking hard.

I *know* Sticks was lying to me, I thought.

I *know* he made the scarecrows move at night. I know he dressed as a scarecrow to scare me in the woods and at the barn. And I know he tossed that scarecrow in front of the horses this morning.

I know he's trying to frighten Mark and me.

But enough is enough, I decided.

Now it's payback time.

Now it's time for *Sticks* to be frightened. Really frightened.

20

"I can't do this!" Mark protested.

"Of course you can," I assured him. "This is going to be really cool."

"But my wrist hurts again," my brother whined. "It just started hurting. I can't use it."

"No problem," I told him. "You won't have to use it."

He started to protest some more. But then a smile spread across his face, and his eyes lit up gleefully. "It's kind of a cool idea," he said, laughing.

"Of *course* it's an awesome idea," I agreed. "*I* thought of it!"

We were standing in the doorway to the barn. The white light from a full moon shone down on us. Owls hooted somewhere nearby.

It was a cool, clear night. The grass shimmered from a heavy dew. A soft wind made the trees whisper. The moonlight was so bright, I could see every blade of grass.

After Grandpa Kurt and Grandma Miriam had gone to bed, I dragged Mark from the house. I pulled him across the yard to the barn.

"Wait right here," I said. Then I hurried into the barn to get what we needed.

It was a little creepy in the dark barn at night. I heard a soft fluttering sound high in the rafters.

Probably a bat.

My sneakers were wet from the grass. I slid over the straw on the barn floor.

The bat swooped low over my head. I heard a high-pitched chittering up in the rafters. More bats.

I grabbed one of the big, old coats from the pile. Then I pulled up one of the burlap bag faces and slung it on top of the coat.

Ignoring the fluttering wings swooping back and forth, back and forth, across the barn, I hurried outside to Mark.

And explained my plan, my plan to get our revenge on Sticks.

It was actually a very simple plan. We'd dress Mark up as a scarecrow. He'd stand with the other scarecrows in the cornfield.

I'd go to the guest house and get Sticks. I'd tell Sticks I saw something weird in the field. I'd pull Sticks out to the field. Mark would start to stagger toward him — and Sticks would be so freaked, he'd have a cow!

A simple plan. And a good one.

Sticks deserved it, too.

I pulled the burlap bag over Mark's head. The black, painted eyes stared back at me. I reached down, picked up a handful of straw, and began stuffing it under the bag.

"Stop squirming!" I told Mark.

"But the straw itches!" he cried.

"You'll get used to it," I told him. I grabbed his shoulders. "Stand still. Don't move."

"Why do I need straw?" he whined.

"Mark, you have to look like all the other scarecrows," I told him. "Otherwise, Sticks won't be fooled."

I stuffed the burlap face with straw. Then I held up the old overcoat for Mark to put on.

"I can't do this!" he wailed. "I'm going to itch to death! I can't breathe!"

"You can breathe perfectly fine," I told him. I stuffed straw into the sleeves. I was careful to let clumps of straw hang from the cuffs, covering Mark's hands. Then I stuffed more straw into the jacket.

"Will you stand still?" I whispered angrily. "This is a lot of hard work — you know?"

He grumbled in a low voice to himself as I continued to work.

"Just keep thinking how great it'll be when Sticks sees you and thinks you're a scarecrow that's really coming to life," I said.

I had straw stuck to my hands, straw all down

the front of my sweatshirt and jeans. I sneezed. Once. Twice. I'm definitely allergic to the stuff.

But I didn't care. I was so excited. I couldn't *wait* to see Sticks's terrified face. I couldn't *wait* to pay him back for trying to frighten us all week.

"I need a hat," Mark said. He was standing stiffly, afraid to move under all the straw.

"Hmmmm." I thought hard. There weren't any hats in the barn with the other scarecrow supplies. "We'll just take one off a real scarecrow," I told Mark.

I stepped back to see my handiwork. Mark looked pretty good. But he still needed more straw. I set to work, stuffing him, making the old coat bulge.

"Now don't forget to stand straight and stiff, with your arms straight out," I instructed.

"Do I have a choice?" Mark complained. "I — I can't move at all!"

"Good," I said. I arranged the straw that stuck out of his sleeves, then stepped back. "Okay. You're ready," I told him.

"How do I look?" he asked.

"Like a short scarecrow," I told him.

"I'm too short?" he replied.

"Don't worry, Mark," I said, grabbing his arm. "I'm going to stick you up on a pole!"

"Huh?"

I laughed. "Gotcha," I muttered. "I'm kidding." I started to lead him to the cornfields.

"Think this is going to work?" Mark asked, walking stiffly. "Think we're really going to scare Sticks?"

I nodded. An evil grin spread over my face. "I think so," I told my brother. "I think Sticks is in for a terrifying surprise."

Little did I know that we *all* were!

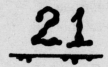

21

I gripped Mark's arm with both hands and led him to the cornfields. The bright moon bathed us in white light. The tall cornstalks shivered in a light breeze.

Mark looked so much like a scarecrow, it was scary. Tufts of straw stuck out at his neck and the cuffs of his coat. The enormous old coat hung loosely over his shoulders and came down nearly to his knees.

We stepped into the field. Our sneakers crunched over the dry ground as we edged through a narrow row.

The cornstalks rose above our heads. The breeze made them lean over us, as if trying to close us in.

I let out a gasp as I heard a rustling sound along the ground.

Footsteps?

Mark and I both froze. And listened.

The tall stalks bent low as the wind picked up. They made an eerie creaking sound as they moved. The ripe corn sheaths bobbed heavily.

Creeeeak. Creeeeak.

The stalks shifted back and forth.

Then we heard the rustling again. A soft brushing sound.

Very nearby.

"Ow. Let go!" Mark whispered.

I suddenly realized I was still gripping his arm, squeezing it tightly.

I let go. And listened. "Do you hear it?" I whispered to Mark. "That brushing sound?"

Creeeeak. Creeeeak.

The cornstalks leaned over us, shifting in the wind.

A twig cracked. So nearby, I nearly jumped out of my skin.

I held my breath. My heart was racing.

Another soft rustling sound. I stared down at the ground, trying to follow the sound.

"Oh."

A large gray squirrel scampered across the row and disappeared between the stalks.

I burst out laughing, mostly from relief. "Just a squirrel," I said. "Do you believe it? Just a squirrel!"

Mark let out a long, relieved sigh from under the burlap bag. "Jodie, can we get going?" he demanded impatiently. "This thing itches like crazy!"

He raised both hands and tried to scratch his face through the bag. But I quickly tugged his arms down. "Mark — stop. You'll mess up the straw!"

"But my face feels like a hundred bugs are crawling all over it!" he wailed. "And I can't see. You didn't cut the eyeholes big enough."

"Just follow me," I muttered. "And stop complaining. You want to scare Sticks, don't you?"

Mark didn't reply. But he let me lead him deeper into the cornfield.

Suddenly, a black shadow fell over our path.

I let out a sharp gasp before I realized it was the long shadow of a scarecrow.

"How do you do," I said, reaching out and shaking its straw hand. "May I borrow your hat?"

I reached up and pulled the brown, floppy hat off the burlap head. Then I lowered it over Mark's burlap head and pulled it down tight.

"Hey — !" Mark protested.

"I don't want it to fall off," I told him.

"I'm never going to stop itching!" Mark whined. "Can you scratch my back? *Please?* My whole back is itching!"

I gave the back of the old coat a few hard rubs. "Turn around," I instructed him. I gave him a final inspection.

Excellent. He looked more like a scarecrow than the scarecrows did.

"Stand right here," I told him, moving him into a small clearing between two rows of cornstalks. "Good. Now when you hear me bringing Sticks over, put your arms straight out. And don't move a muscle."

"I know, I know," Mark grumbled. "Think I don't know how to be a scarecrow? Just hurry — okay?"

"Okay," I told him. I turned and made my way quickly along the shifting rows of cornstalks. Dry straw and leaves crackled beneath my sneakers.

I was breathing hard by the time I reached the guest house. The doorway was dark. But an orange light glowed dimly behind the pulled shade in the window.

I hesitated at the doorway and listened. Silence inside.

How was I going to get Sticks to come out alone — without his father?

I didn't want to frighten Stanley. He was a really nice man, who would never think of playing mean jokes on Mark and me. And I knew how scared and upset he could get.

I only wanted to frighten Sticks. To teach him a lesson. To teach him he had no business getting on our case just because Mark and I are "city kids."

The wind fluttered through my hair. I could hear the cornstalks creaking behind me in the fields.

I shivered.

Taking a deep breath, I raised my fist to knock on the door.

But a sound behind me made me spin around.

"Hey — !" I choked out.

Someone was moving across the grass, half running, half stumbling. My eyes were all watery. It was hard to see.

Was it Mark?

Yes. I recognized the floppy hat, the bulky, dark overcoat falling down past his knees.

What is he doing? I asked myself, watching him approach.

Why is he following me?

He's going to ruin the whole joke!

As he came closer, he raised a straw hand as if pointing at me.

"Mark — what's wrong?" I called in a loud whisper.

He continued to gesture with his straw hand as he ran.

"Mark — get back in the field!" I whispered. "You're not supposed to follow me. You're going to ruin everything! Mark — what are you *doing* here?"

I motioned with both hands for him to go back to the cornfield.

But he ignored me and kept coming, trailing straw as he ran.

"Mark, please — go back! Go back!" I pleaded.

But he stepped up in front of me and grabbed my shoulders.

And as I stared into the cold, painted black eyes — I realized to my horror that *it wasn't Mark!*

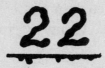

22

I cried out and tried to pull away.

But the scarecrow held on to me tightly.

"Sticks — is that you?" I cried in a trembling voice.

No reply.

I stared into the blank, painted eyes.

And realized there were no human eyes behind them.

The straw hands scratched against my throat.

I opened my mouth to scream.

And the door to the guest house swung open. "Sticks — " I managed to choke out.

Sticks stepped out onto the small stoop. "What on earth — !" he cried.

He leaped off the stoop, grabbed the scarecrow by the coat shoulders — and heaved it to the ground.

The scarecrow hit the ground without making a sound. It lay sprawled on its back, staring up at us blankly.

"Who — who is it?" I cried, rubbing my neck where the straw hands had scratched it.

Sticks bent down and jerked away the burlap scarecrow head.

Nothing underneath. Nothing but straw.

"It — it really is a scarecrow!" I cried in horror. "But it — *walked!*"

"I warned you," Sticks said solemnly, staring down at the headless dark figure. "I warned you, Jodie."

"You mean it wasn't you?" I demanded. "It wasn't you trying to scare Mark and me?"

Sticks shook his head. He raised his dark eyes to mine. "Dad brought the scarecrows to life," he said softly. "Last week. Before you came. He used his book. He chanted some words — and they all came to life."

"Oh, no," I murmured, raising my hands to my face.

"We were all so frightened," Sticks continued. "Especially your grandparents. They begged Dad to recite the words and put the scarecrows back to sleep."

"Did he?" I asked.

"Yes," Sticks replied. "He put them back to sleep. But first he insisted your grandparents make some promises. They had to promise not to laugh at him anymore. And they had to promise to do everything he wanted from now on."

Sticks took a deep breath. He stared toward

the guest house window. "Haven't you noticed how different things are at the farm? Haven't you noticed how frightened your grandparents are?"

I nodded solemnly. "Of course I have."

"They've been trying to keep Dad happy," Sticks continued. "They've been doing everything they can to keep him from getting upset or angry. Your grandmother fixes only his favorite food. Your grandfather stopped telling scary stories because Dad doesn't like them."

I shook my head. "They're *that* afraid of Stanley?"

"They're afraid he'll read the chant in the book again and bring the scarecrows back to life," Sticks said. He swallowed hard. "There's only one problem," he murmured.

"What's that?" I asked.

"Well, I haven't told Dad yet. But . . ." His voice trailed off.

"But what?" I demanded eagerly.

"Some of the scarecrows are still alive," Sticks replied. "Some of them never went back to sleep."

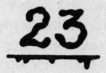

23

We both let out short cries as the front door to the house swung open.

Startled, I leaped away from the doorway.

As the door pulled open, it revealed a rectangle of orange light. Stanley stepped into the light.

He held on to the door and peered out. His eyes showed surprise as they landed on Sticks and me. But then he goggled and uttered a choking sound as he spotted the headless scarecrow on the ground.

"N-no!" Stanley sputtered. He pointed a trembling finger at the scarecrow. "It — it walks! The scarecrow walks!"

"No, Dad — !" Sticks cried.

But Stanley didn't hear him. Stanley had already dived back into the house.

Sticks started after him. But Stanley reappeared in the doorway. As he stepped outside, I saw that he was carrying the big superstition book.

"The scarecrows walk!" Stanley screamed. "I must take charge! I must take charge of them all now!"

His eyes were wild. His entire skinny body was trembling. He started toward the cornfields, totally crazy. Sticks tried to calm him down.

"No, Dad!" Sticks cried desperately, hurrying after him. "The scarecrow was dropped here! I dropped it here, Dad! It didn't walk! It didn't walk!"

Stanley kept walking, taking long, rapid strides. He didn't seem to hear Sticks. "I must take charge now!" Stanley declared. "I must be the leader. I will bring the others back to life and take control."

He turned and glanced at Sticks, who was hurrying to catch up to him. "Stay back!" Stanley shouted. "Stay back — until I read the chant! Then you can follow!"

"Dad — please listen to me!" Sticks cried. "The scarecrows are all asleep! Don't wake them!"

Stanley finally stopped a few yards from the edge of the cornfields. He turned to Sticks and studied his face. "You're sure? You're sure they're not out of my control? You're sure they're not walking?"

Sticks nodded. "Yes. I'm sure, Dad. I'm really sure."

Stanley's face filled with confusion. He kept staring hard at Sticks, as if not believing him. "I don't have to read the chant?" Stanley asked, confused, his eyes on the swaying cornstalks. "I don't have to take charge?"

"No, Dad," Sticks replied softly. "The scarecrows are all still. You can put the book away. The scarecrows are not moving."

Stanley sighed with relief. He lowered the book to his side. "None of them?" he asked warily.

"None of them," Sticks replied soothingly.

And that's when Mark — in full scarecrow costume — decided to come staggering out of the cornfield.

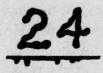

24

"Where've you been?" Mark called.

Stanley's eyes went wide, and he opened his mouth in a high shriek of terror.

"Dad, please — !" Sticks pleaded.

Too late.

Stanley took off, heading into the cornfields, the big book raised high in front of him. "The scarecrows walk! They walk!" he cried.

Mark tucked at the burlap bag face. "Did we blow it?" he called. "Is the joke over? What's happening?"

There was no time to answer him.

Sticks turned to me, his features tight with fear. "We've got to stop Dad!" he cried. He started running to the swaying cornstalks.

Stanley had already disappeared between the tall rows of corn.

My allergies were really bad. I kept rubbing my eyes, trying to clear them. But as I followed

Sticks, everything was a shimmering blur of grays and blacks.

"Ow!" I cried out as I stumbled in a soft hole and fell.

Mark, right behind me, nearly toppled over me.

He reached down and helped pull me up. I had landed hard on both knees, and they were throbbing with pain.

"Which way did they go?" I asked breathlessly, searching the dark, swaying rows of creaking cornstalks.

"I — I'm not sure!" Mark stammered. "What's going on, Jodie? Tell me!"

"Not now!" I told him. "We have to stop Stanley. We have to — "

Stanley's voice, high and excited, rose up from somewhere nearby. Mark and I both froze as we listened to the strange words he was chanting.

"Is he reading something from that weird book?" Mark demanded.

Without answering, I headed in the direction of Stanley's voice. It was easy to follow him. He was chanting the strange words at the top of his lungs.

Where was Sticks? I wondered.

Why hadn't Sticks been able to stop his father?

I pushed frantically through the tall stalks. I was moving blindly, my eyes watered over, brushing the stalks out of the way with both hands.

In a small clearing, I found Stanley and Sticks. They were standing in front of two scarecrows on poles.

Stanley held the book up close to his face as he chanted, moving his finger over the words.

Sticks stood frozen, a blank expression on his face, a face of cold terror.

Had the words of the chant somehow frozen him there like that?

The scarecrows stood stiffly on their poles, their painted eyes staring lifelessly out from under their floppy black hats.

Mark and I stepped into the clearing just as Stanley finished his chant. He slammed the big book shut and tucked it under one arm.

"They're going to walk now!" Stanley cried excitedly. "They're going to come alive again!"

Sticks suddenly seemed to come back to life. He blinked several times and shook his head hard, as if trying to clear it.

We all stared at the two scarecrows.

They stared back at us, lifeless, unmoving.

The clouds floated away from the moon. The shadow over the cornfields rolled away.

I stared into the eerie, pale light.

A heavy silence descended over us. The only sounds I could hear were Stanley's shallow breathing, tense gasps as he waited for his chant to work, for his scarecrows to come to life.

I don't know how long we stood there, none of

us moving a muscle, watching the scarecrows. Watching. Watching.

"It didn't work," Stanley moaned finally. His voice came out sad and low. "I did something wrong. The chant — it didn't work."

A smile grew on Sticks's face. He gazed at me. "It didn't work!" Sticks exclaimed happily.

And then I heard the *scratch scratch scratch* of dry straw.

I saw the scarecrows' shoulders start to twitch. I saw their eyes light up and their heads lean forward.

Scratch scratch scratch.

The dry straw crinkled loudly as they both squirmed off their poles and lowered themselves silently to the ground.

25

"Go warn your grandparents!" Sticks cried. "Hurry! Go tell them what my dad has done!"

Mark and I hesitated. We stared at the scarecrows as they stretched their arms and rolled their burlap bag heads, as if waking up after a long sleep.

"Jodie — look!" Mark choked out in a hushed whisper. He pointed out to the fields.

I gasped in horror as I saw what Mark was staring at.

All over the field, dark-coated scarecrows were stretching, squirming, lowering themselves from their poles.

More than a dozen of them, silently coming to life.

"Run!" Sticks was screaming. "Go! Tell your grandparents!"

Stanley stood frozen in place, gripping the book in both hands. He stared in amazement, shaking his head, enjoying his triumph.

Sticks's face was knotted with fear. He gave my shoulders a hard shove. "Run!"

The scarecrows were rolling their heads back and forth, stretching out their straw arms. The dry scratch of straw filled the night air.

I forced myself to take my eyes off them. Mark and I turned and started running through the cornfield. We pushed the tall stalks away with both hands as we ran. We ducked our heads low, running in terrified silence.

We ran across the grass, past the guest house. Past the dark, silent barn.

The farmhouse loomed darkly ahead of us. The windows were dark. A dim porch light sent a circle of yellow light over the back porch.

"Hey — !" Mark shouted, pointing.

Grandpa Kurt and Grandma Miriam must have heard our shouts back in the cornfields. They were waiting for us in the back yard.

They looked frail and frightened. Grandma Miriam had pulled a flannel bathrobe over her nightdress. She had a scarf tied over her short red hair.

Grandpa Kurt had pulled his overalls on over his pajamas. He leaned heavily on his cane, shaking his head as Mark and I came running up.

"The scarecrows — !" I exclaimed breathlessly.

"They're walking!" Mark cried. "Stanley — he — "

"Did you get Stanley upset?" Grandpa Kurt asked, his eyes wide with fear. "Who got Stanley upset? He promised us he wouldn't do it again! He promised — if we didn't upset him."

"It was an accident!" I told him. "We didn't mean to. Really!"

"We've worked so hard to keep Stanley happy," Grandma Miriam said sadly. She chewed her lower lip. "So hard . . ."

"I didn't think he'd do it," Grandpa Kurt said, his eyes on the cornfields. "I thought we convinced him it was too dangerous."

"Why are you dressed like that?" Grandma Miriam asked Mark.

I was so frightened and upset, I had completely forgotten that Mark was still dressed as a scarecrow.

"Mark, did you dress like that to scare Stanley?" Grandma Miriam demanded.

"No!" Mark cried. "It was supposed to be a joke! Just a joke!"

"We were trying to scare Sticks," I told them. "But when Stanley saw Mark, he . . ."

My voice trailed off as I saw the dark figures step out of the cornfields.

In the silvery moonlight, I saw Stanley and Sticks. They were running hard, leaning forward as they ran. Stanley held the book in front of him. His shoes slipped and slid over the wet grass.

Behind them came the scarecrows. They were moving awkwardly, staggering, lurching silently forward.

Their straw arms stretched straight forward, as if reaching to grab Stanley and Sticks. Their round, black eyes glowed blankly in the moonlight.

Staggering, tumbling, falling, they came after Stanley and Sticks. A dozen twisted figures in black coats and hats. Leaving clumps of straw as they pulled themselves forward.

Grandma Miriam grabbed my arm and squeezed it in terror. Her hand was as cold as ice.

We watched Stanley fall, then scramble to his feet. Sticks helped pull him up, and the two of them continued to run toward us in terror.

The silent scarecrows lurched and staggered closer. Closer.

"Help us — *please!*" Stanley called to us.

"What can we do?" I heard Grandpa Kurt mutter sadly.

26

The four of us huddled close together, staring in helpless horror as the scarecrows made their way, chasing Stanley and Sticks across the moonlit lawn.

Grandma Miriam held on to my arm. Grandpa Kurt leaned heavily, squeezing the handle of his cane.

"They won't obey me!" Stanley screamed breathlessly. He stopped in front of us, holding the book in one hand.

His chest was heaving up and down as he struggled to catch his breath. Despite the coolness of the night, sweat poured down his forehead.

"They won't obey me! They *must* obey me! The book says so!" Stanley cried, frantically waving the book in the air.

Sticks stopped beside his father. He turned to watch the scarecrows approach. "What are you going to do?" he asked his father. "You *have* to do something!"

"They're alive!" Stanley shrieked. "Alive!"

"What does the book say?" Grandpa Kurt demanded.

"They're alive! They're all alive!" Stanley repeated, his eyes wild with fright.

"Stanley — listen to me!" Grandpa Kurt yelled. He grabbed Stanley by the shoulders and spun him around to face him. "Stanley — what does the book say to do? How do you get them in control?"

"Alive," Stanley murmured, his eyes rolling in his head. "They're all alive."

"Stanley — what does the book say to do?" Grandpa Kurt demanded once again.

"I — I don't know," Stanley replied.

We turned back to the scarecrows. They were moving closer. Spreading out. Forming a line as they staggered toward us. Their arms reached forward menacingly, as if preparing to grab us.

Clumps of straw fell from their sleeves. Straw spilled from their coats.

But they continued to lurch toward us. Closer. Closer.

The black, painted eyes stared straight ahead. They leered at us with their ugly, painted mouths.

"Stop!" Stanley screamed, raising the book high over his head. "I command you to stop!"

The scarecrows lurched slowly, steadily forward.

"Stop!" Stanley shrieked in a high, frightened

111

voice. "I brought you to life! You are mine! Mine! I command you! I command you to stop!"

The blank eyes stared straight at us. The arms reached stiffly forward. The scarecrows pulled themselves closer. Closer.

"Stop! I said *stop*!" Stanley screeched.

Mark edged closer to me. Behind his burlap mask I could see his eyes. Terrified eyes.

Ignoring Stanley's frightened pleas, the scarecrows dragged themselves closer. Closer.

And then I did something that changed the whole night.

I sneezed.

27

Mark was so startled by my sudden, loud sneeze that he let out a short cry and jumped away from me.

To my amazement, the scarecrows all stopped moving forward — and jumped back, too.

"Whoa!" I cried. "What's going on here?"

The scarecrows all seemed to have trained their painted eyes on Mark.

"Mark — quick — raise your right hand!" I cried.

Mark gazed at me through the burlap bag. I could see confusion in his eyes.

But he obediently raised his right hand high over his head.

And the scarecrows all raised *their* right hands!

"Mark — they're imitating you!" Grandma Miriam cried.

Mark raised *both* hands in the air.

The scarecrows copied him again. I heard the scratch of straw as they lifted both arms.

Mark tilted his head to the left. The scarecrows tilted their heads to the left.

Mark dropped to his knees. The scarecrows sank in their straw, slaves to my brother's every move.

"They — they think you're one of them," Grandpa Kurt whispered.

"They think you're their *leader*!" Stanley cried, staring wide-eyed at the scarecrows slumped on the ground.

"But how do I make them go back to their poles?" Mark demanded excitedly. "How do I make them go back to being scarecrows?"

"Dad — find the right chant!" Sticks yelled. "Find the right words! Make them sleep again!"

Stanley scratched his short, dark hair. "I — I'm too scared!" he confessed sadly.

And then I had an idea.

"Mark — " I whispered, leaning close to him. "Pull off your head."

"Huh?" He gazed at me through the burlap mask.

"Pull off your scarecrow head," I urged him, still whispering.

"But why?" Mark demanded. He waved his hands in the air. The scarecrows obediently waved their straw hands in the air.

Everyone was staring at me, eager to hear my explanation.

"If you pull off your scarecrow head," I told

Mark, "then they will pull off *their* heads. And they'll die."

Mark hesitated. "Huh? You think so?"

"It's worth a try," Grandpa Kurt urged.

"Go ahead, Mark. Hurry!" Sticks cried.

Mark hesitated for a second. Then he stepped forward, just inches from the dark-coated scarecrows.

"Hurry!" Sticks urged him.

Mark gripped the top of the burlap bag with both hands. "I sure hope this works," he murmured. Then he gave the bag a hard tug and pulled it off.

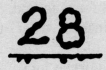

28

The scarecrows stopped moving. They stood still as statues as they watched Mark pull off his scarecrow head.

Mark stared back at them, holding the burlap bag between his hands. His hair was matted wetly to his forehead. He was dripping with sweat.

The scarecrows hesitated for a moment more.

A long, silent moment.

I held my breath. My heart was pounding.

Then I let out a happy cry as the scarecrows all reached up with their straw hands — and pulled off their heads!

The dark hats and burlap heads fell silently to the grass.

None of us moved. We were waiting for the scarecrows to fall.

Waiting for the headless scarecrows to collapse and fall.

But they didn't go down.

Instead, they reached out their arms and moved stiffly, menacingly forward.

"They — they're coming to get us!" Stanley cried in a high, trembling voice.

"Mark — *do* something!" I shouted, shoving him forward. "Make them stand on one foot or hop up and down. Stop them!"

The headless figures dragged themselves toward us, arms outstretched.

Mark stepped forward. He raised both hands over his head.

The scarecrows didn't stop, didn't copy him.

"Hey — hands up!" Mark shouted desperately. He waved his hands above his head.

The scarecrows edged forward, silently, steadily.

"Th-they're not doing it!" Mark wailed. "They're not *following* me!"

"You don't look like a scarecrow anymore," Grandma Miriam added. "They don't think you're their leader."

Closer they came, staggering blindly. Closer.

They formed a tight circle around us.

A scarecrow brushed its straw hand against my cheek.

I uttered a terrified cry. "Noooooo!"

It reached for my throat, the dry straw scratching me, scratching my face, scratching, scratching.

The headless scarecrows swarmed over Mark. He thrashed and kicked. But they were smothering him, forcing him to the ground.

My grandparents cried out helplessly as the dark-coated figures surrounded them. Stanley let out a silent gasp.

"Sticks — help me!" I shrieked as the straw hands wrapped around my neck. "Sticks? Sticks?"

I glanced frantically around.

"Sticks? Help me! Please! Where are you?"

Then I realized to my horror that Sticks was gone.

29

"Sticks?" I let out a final muffled cry.

The straw hands wrapped around my throat. The scarecrow rolled over me. My face was pressed into the dry straw of its chest.

I tried to squirm free. But it held on, surrounded me, choked me.

The straw smelled sour. Decayed. I felt sick. A wave of nausea swept over me.

"Let go! Let go!" I heard Stanley pleading.

The scarecrow was surprisingly strong. It wrapped its arms around me tightly, smothering me in the disgusting straw.

I made one last attempt to pull free. Struggling with all my might, I raised my head.

And saw two balls of fire. Orange streaks of light.

Floating closer.

And in the orange light, I saw Sticks's face, hard and determined.

I gave another hard tug. And tumbled backwards.

"Sticks!" I cried.

He was carrying two blazing torches. The torches from the barn, I realized.

"I was saving these just in case!" Sticks called.

The scarecrows seemed to sense danger.

They let go of us, tried to scramble away.

But Sticks moved quickly.

He swept the two torches, swinging them like baseball bats.

A scarecrow caught fire. Then another.

Sticks made another wide swing.

The fire crackled, a streak of orange against the darkness.

The dry straw burst into flame. The old coats burned quickly.

The scarecrows twisted and writhed as the bright flames danced over them. They sank to their backs on the ground. Burning. Burning so brightly, so silently, so fast.

I took a step back, staring in horror and fascination.

Grandpa Kurt had his arm around Grandma Miriam. They leaned close together, their faces reflecting the flickering flames.

Stanley stood tensely, his eyes wide. He hugged the book tightly to his chest. He was murmuring to himself, but I couldn't make out the words.

Mark and I stood beside Sticks, who held a torch

in each hand, watching with narrowed eyes as the scarecrows burned.

In seconds, there was nothing left but clumps of dark ashes on the ground.

"It's over," Grandma Miriam murmured softly, gratefully.

"Never again," I heard Stanley mutter.

The house was quiet the next afternoon.

Mark was out on the screen porch, lying in the hammock, reading a stack of comic books. Grandpa Kurt and Grandma Miriam had gone in for their afternoon nap.

Sticks had driven into town to pick up the mail.

Stanley sat at the kitchen table, reading his superstition book. His finger moved over the page as he muttered the words aloud in a low voice.

"Never again," he had repeated at lunch. "I've learned my lesson about this book. I'll never try to bring any scarecrows to life again. I won't even *read* the part about scarecrows!"

We were all glad to hear that.

So now, on this lazy, peaceful afternoon, Stanley sat at the table, quietly reading some chapter of the big book.

And I sat alone on the couch in the living room, hearing Stanley's gentle murmurings from the kitchen, thinking about the night before.

It felt good to have a quiet afternoon, to be all alone to think about what had happened.

All alone . . .

The only one in the room . . .

The only one to hear Stanley's low mumbling as he read the book.

The only one to see the gigantic stuffed brown bear blink its eyes.

The only one to see the bear lick its lips, step off its platform, snarl and paw the air with its enormous claws.

The only one to hear its stomach growl as it stared down at me.

The only one to see the hungry look on its face as it magically came out of its long hibernation.

"Stanley?" I called in a tiny, high voice. "Stanley? What chapter have you been reading?"

Add *more*

Goosebumps

to your collection . . .
A chilling preview of
what's next from
R.L. STINE

GO EAT WORMS!

4

Todd walked over to the window and peered out, pressing his nose against the glass. "What is Patrick MacKay doing in my worm-digging spot?" he demanded angrily.

Danny stepped beside Todd. He squinted out into the gray afternoon. "Are you sure that's Patrick MacKay?"

The sky darkened as the low clouds gathered. The boy on the playground was half covered by shadow. But Todd recognized him anyway.

That snobby, stuck-up, rich kid. Patrick MacKay.

He was bent over the bare spot of mud behind second base, working feverishly.

"What is he *doing* out there?" Todd repeated. "That's my best worm spot!"

"He's digging up worms, too!" Regina declared from the table.

"Huh?" Todd spun around to find his sister smirking at him.

"Patrick is digging up worms for the Science Expo," she told him, unable to hide her joy. "He's doing a worm project, too."

"But he *can't!*" Todd sputtered in a high, shrill voice.

"Whoa! What a copycat!" Danny declared.

"He can't do a worm project! *I'm* doing the worm project!" Todd insisted, turning back to stare at Patrick through the glass.

"It's a free country," Regina replied smugly. She and Beth laughed and slapped each other high fives. They were enjoying seeing Todd squirm for a change.

"But he's not into worms!" Todd continued, very upset. "He doesn't collect worms! He doesn't study worms! He's just copying me!"

"Look at him, digging in your spot," Danny murmured, shaking his head bitterly.

"Patrick is a nice guy," Beth remarked. "He doesn't act like a jerk and put worms in people's soup."

"He's a jerk," Todd insisted angrily, staring hard out the window. "He's a total jerk."

"He's a copycat jerk," Danny added.

"His worm project is going to be better than yours," Regina teased him.

Todd's dark eyes burned into his sister's. "You know what it is? You know what Patrick's project is?"

Regina had a smug smile on her lips. She tossed

back her brown hair. Then she made a zipper sign, moving her fingers across her lips. "I'll never tell," she said.

"What is it?" Todd demanded. "Tell me."

Regina shook her head.

"Tell me, Beth," Todd insisted, narrowing his eyes menacingly at Beth.

"No way," Beth replied, glancing merrily at Regina.

"Then I'll ask him myself," Todd declared. "Come on, Danny."

The two boys started running through the lunchroom. They were nearly to the door when Todd ran into their teacher.

Miss Grant was carrying her lunch tray high over her head, stepping around a group of kids in the aisle. Todd just didn't see her.

He bumped her from behind.

She uttered a cry of surprise — and her tray flew out of her hands. The tray and the plates clattered loudly onto the floor. And her food — salad and a bowl of spaghetti — dropped around her feet.

"What is your hurry, young man?" she snapped at Todd.

"Uh . . . sorry," Todd murmured. It was the only reply he could think of.

Miss Grant bent to examine her brown shoes, which were now orange, covered with wet clumps of spaghetti.

"It was an accident," Todd said impatiently, fiddling with his Raiders cap.

"It sure was," the teacher replied coldly. "Perhaps I should speak to you after school about why we don't run in the lunchroom?"

"Perhaps," Todd agreed. Then he bolted past her, running out the door faster than he had ever run.

"Cool move, ace!" Danny exclaimed, running beside him.

"It wasn't my fault," Todd told him. "She stepped in front of me."

"The bell is going to ring," Danny warned as they made their way out the back door.

"I don't care," Todd replied breathlessly. "I've got to find out what that copycat is doing with worms!"

Patrick was still bent over the mud behind second base. He was scooping up worms with a silvery trowel that looked brand-new, then dropping them into a metal bait can.

He was a slim, good-looking boy with wavy blond hair and blue eyes. He had started school in September. His family had moved to Ohio from Pasadena. He was always telling everyone how California was so much better.

He didn't brag about how rich he was. But he wore designer jeans, and his mother brought him to school every morning in a long, white Lincoln.

So Todd and the others at William Tecumseh Sherman Middle School figured it out.

Patrick was in Regina's class. A few weeks after school started, he had a big birthday party and invited everyone in his class. Including Regina.

She reported that Patrick had a whole carnival, with rides and everything in his back yard. Todd pretended he didn't care that he wasn't invited.

The sky grew even darker as Danny and Todd stood over Patrick on the playground. "What are you doing, Patrick?" Todd demanded.

"Digging," Patrick replied, glancing up from his work.

"Digging up worms?" Todd asked, his hands pressed against the waist of his jeans.

Patrick nodded. He started digging again. He pulled up a long, dark brown one that Todd would have loved to own.

"*I'm* doing a worm project," Todd told him.

"I know," Patrick replied, concentrating on his work. "Me, too."

"What is it?" Danny chimed in. "What's your project, Patrick?"

Patrick didn't reply. He dug up a tiny, pale worm, examined it, and tossed it back.

"What's your project? Tell us," Todd demanded.

"You really want to know?" Patrick asked, raising his blue eyes to them. The wind ruffled his blond hair, but the hair immediately fell back into place.

Todd felt a raindrop on his shoulder. Then one on the top of his head.

"What's your project?" Todd repeated.

"Okay, okay," Patrick said, wiping dirt off his hands. "I'll tell you. My project is . . . "

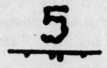

5

The class bell rang. The sharp clang cut through the rising wind. The rain started to patter loudly against the ground.

"We've got to go in," Danny urged, tugging at Todd's sleeve.

"Wait," Todd said, his eyes on Patrick. "Tell me now!" he insisted.

"But we'll be late!" Danny insisted, tugging at Todd again. "And we're getting soaked."

Patrick climbed to his feet. "I think I've got all the worms I need." He shook wet dirt off the silvery trowel.

"So what is your worm project?" Todd repeated, ignoring the pattering rain and Danny's urgent requests to get back inside the school.

Patrick grinned at him, revealing about three hundred perfect white teeth. "I'm teaching them to fly," he said.

"Huh?"

"I'm putting cardboard wings on them and

teaching them to fly. Wait till you see it! It's a riot!" He burst out laughing.

Danny leaned close to Todd. "Is he for real?" he whispered.

"Of course not!" Todd shot back. "Don't be a jerk, Danny. He's goofing on us."

"Hey — you're not funny," Danny told Patrick angrily.

"We're late, guys. Let's get going," Patrick said, his grin fading. He started toward the school building.

But Todd moved quickly to block his path. "Tell me the truth, Patrick. What are you planning to do?"

Patrick started to reply.

But a low rumbling sound made him stop.

They all heard it. A muffled roar that made the ground shake.

The worm can fell out of Patrick's hand. His blue eyes opened wide in surprise — and fear.

The rumbling gave way to a loud, cracking noise. It sounded as if the whole playground were splitting apart.

"Wh-what's *happening*?" Patrick stammered.

"Run!" Todd screamed as the ground trembled and shook. "Run for your life!"

About the Author

R.L. STINE is the author of over two dozen best-selling thrillers and mysteries for young people. Recent titles for teenagers include *Call Waiting*, *Halloween Night*, *The Dead Girlfriend*, and *The Baby-sitter III*, all published by Scholastic. He is also the author of the *Fear Street* series.

When he isn't writing scary books, he is head writer of the children's TV show *Eureeka's Castle*, seen on Nickelodeon.

Bob lives in New York City with his wife, Jane, and fourteen-year-old son, Matt.

GET
Goosebumps
by R.L. Stine

Scare me, thrill me, mail me GOOSEBUMPS Now!

Available wherever you buy books, or use this order form. Scholastic Inc., P.O. Box 7502,
2931 East McCarty Street, Jefferson City, MO 65102

Please send me the books I have checked above. I am enclosing $_____ (please add
$2.00 to cover shipping and handling). Send check or money order — no cash or C.O.D.s please.

Name _____ Age _____

Address _____

City _____ State/Zip _____

Please allow four to six weeks for delivery. Offer good in the U.S. only. Sorry, mail orders are not available to
residents of Canada. Prices subject to change.

GB53095